why me?

CHIMERAS, CONUNDRUMS AND DEAD GOLDFISH

CHARLOTTE STUART

Praise for *Why Me? Chimeras, Conundrums and Dead Goldfish*

"Fans of the classic cozy mystery genre are sure to adore the work of author Charlotte Stuart, whose quintessentially quirky cast and premise already set the story up as a winner from the start."
—K.C. Finn, Readers' Favorite

"Charming heroine, handsome cat, helpful men, and a puzzling mystery. A perfect read."
—Dorothyanne Brown, Reedsy

"Charlotte Stuart has a gift for mystery writing with plenty of humor and flawed characters. This was my first book by her and let me tell you, I will be reading more."
—N. N. Light's Book Heaven

"I love the way Charlotte Stuart writes her main characters. I embrace them as my friends right away."
—Christy's Cozy Corners Review

"*Why Me? Chimeras, Conundrums and Dead Goldfish* by Charlotte Stuart has an unusual title and an equally unusual and interesting murder/mystery to go along with it."
—Grant Leishman, Readers' Favorite

"This is a delightful and quirky new mystery and it will definitely keep you on your toes . . . I think this is going to make an interesting series and I can't wait to see what is on tap next for Bryn and the gang."
—StoryBook Reviews

"Full of fascinating characters, crafty clues, and a few unexpected twists that make it a great read for cozy mystery fans."
—Books a Plenty Book Reviews

To my late mother and my Aunt Sarol
for sharing their sense of humor.

Chimera research is highly controversial. It has the potential to save countless lives each year through biomedical treatments such as growing human organs in animals, but it raises serious bioethical questions. The NIH has established policies to regulate certain types of research funded by NIH, but that doesn't begin to address the qualms of many scientists and concerned members of the public in the US. The international community is also divided on what research should and should not be legal. In China, for example, some scientists are experimenting with the implantation of human genes into the brain cells of rhesus monkeys. Many adamantly oppose this kind of research because they believe it blurs the lines between animals and humans. At what point does an intelligent animal acquire rights similar to humans? This human-animal moral dilemma is the subject of numerous journal articles and discussions. As are concerns about the treatment of animals in medical research. Unfortunately, the bioethics issues raised are a long way from being resolved by consistent guidelines and regulations.

Finally, my apologies to the midges of Scotland for how they are portrayed in this book, even though they are truly annoying.

Science cannot stop while ethics catches up.
Elvin Stakman, American plant pathologist

Dilbert: *Wow! According to my computer simulation, it should be possible to create new life forms from common household chemicals.*
Dogbert: *This raises some thorny issues.*
Dilbert: *You mean legal, ethical and religious issues?*
Dogbert: *I was thinking about parking spaces.*

the midges and me

It was like standing under a waterfall. My rain hat was battered down around my ears by the plus size raindrops. Water plunged off the rim, struck the front of my poncho, and pinged back up at my face. Both my shoes and my spirits were not just dampened, but sodden. Water cascaded down my rain pants, bypassed my trail gaiters, and went directly into my hiking boots. Once inside, it did not seep out. Not quite what I'd had in mind when I'd purchased the expensive waterproof footwear.

To top it off, I was surrounded by a swarm of midges, tiny vampire bugs that had no business being out in a downpour. They hung there, inches from my face, waiting for my DEET to wash off. One thing for sure, I wouldn't be sending any selfies back to friends from *this* hike.

I had definitely chosen the wrong friend and the wrong season for a hiking trip to Scotland. Sophie's been my best friend since high school. She and I had decided it would be fun to explore some remote hills and lochs in Scotland, maybe venture into the Highlands region. We'd planned to spend most of our time on day hikes, staying in what we envisioned to be quaint villages along the way. We had our passports in hand, our reservations set, our schedules adjusted, pet care arranged, and I had even purchased a satellite communicator with 100% global coverage. But at the last minute, Sophie wanted to postpone. Why? Because Sophie has men issues.

When we were younger Sophie went through men like there was an endless supply. She didn't have a "type." She liked variety. After a disastrous marriage in her twenties, she went back to playing the field. I gave up trying to remember names and labeled each one "Sophie's latest." That continued into our thirties, until she hit thirty-five. Then she started looking for "the" one, the one she intended to spend the rest of her life with. And, unfortunately, she met her most recent potentially perfect someone a week before we were scheduled to take off on our adventure, and she didn't want to risk leaving during this "critical time" in their relationship. She was sorry and hoped I understood. I did, but I was also angry. So, I damn well decided to go on the trip without her.

How was I to know Scotland had a midge season? Sophie had done most of the planning. Not only had she failed to mention the midges, she had also omitted the fact that we would be hiking in an area the guidebook referred to as "one of the wettest places in Scotland." Okay, so I should have helped more with the itinerary. But Sophie is a take-charge kind of woman, and I'd been more than happy to let her handle the details.

So, there I was, hiking by myself in the rain, regretting that I hadn't had the good sense to read the guidebooks *before* I'd hopped on the plane.

After slogging up a steep incline for about fifteen minutes, I stopped to catch my breath at the edge of a deep, narrow ravine. Although the landscape seemed barren compared to what I was used to back home, the hillside was covered with a tangle of bracken and plush groundcovers. At the bottom a few stunted looking trees hugged a stream that ran through the middle of the gorge and disappeared around a bend to my left. Directly below were some huge boulders that looked like they had been tossed there by a giant as ravine art.

There was also something else down there. Something that didn't quite belong.

I blinked the rainwater out of my eyes and peered through the veil of bugs. Just this side of one of the large boulders was something that looked suspiciously . . . like a person. A person sprawled on the ground. And the angle of repose did not look natural.

"Dammit," I said. Why me? Why had I stopped and looked down at those boulders? Now I was morally bound to find out what or who I was looking at. But dammit all, the last thing I wanted to do in a downpour was climb down a steep hillside to check out what could turn out to be a pile of clothes someone had tossed over the edge. On the other hand, if that *was* a person down there, they were either injured or dead. That was certainly a lot worse than being wet and buggy.

On the off chance there were fellow hikers nearby, I shouted: "Anybody there? Can anyone hear me?"

Not surprisingly, no one responded. I hadn't seen another human being since I left the car park. Even the car park had been nearly empty. Anyone with an ounce of sense was safely in their home or a hotel room or in a pub, relaxing in a comfortable chair, dry and warm, with the midges hovering *outside* instead of scant inches away. There wasn't anyone else; it was all up to me. I had to find a way down. And clearly it wasn't going to be easy. Perhaps even dangerous. I could fall and end up next to whoever or whatever it was down there.

Damn, damn, damn. *Why me* I asked myself again.

Before starting the descent, I checked my cell just to verify there was no reception. It didn't really matter; there was no one to call for advice, and I had a satellite communicator. But I didn't want to use my satellite communicator until I knew what kind of help was needed, if any. If my "person" turned out to be a dump site, I wouldn't need to call the Mountain Rescue Team. And if there was an actual person down there, I needed to know what the situation was before making the call.

I'd already broken cardinal rule #1—never hike alone in an isolated area. Now I was about to break rule #2 – always stay on well-defined paths. But what choice did I have?

Reluctantly, I started down on a traverse, as if I were skiing instead of making my way through a mass of slippery rocks and wet foliage. In my head I could hear my mother's voice telling me that you didn't avoid doing the right thing just because it was difficult. "All right, Mom," I said as I waved my arms to ward off the midges. "I'm on my way."

Slowly, I angled back and forth, clinging to any shrubs that I didn't trip on, using the occasional rock to keep from sliding sideways. My thighs protested against the strain of maintaining my balance on the steep slope, but I somehow managed to stay on my feet and make slow but steady progress.

It seemed to take forever. The midges hovered even closer, as if preparing to devour my corpse as soon as the opportunity presented itself. I was so relieved to finally reach the bottom that I relaxed my vigilance too soon and promptly caught the toe of my shoe on a vine, falling face first in some moss studded with brambles. It's surprising how hard moss can be with a 25-pound pack pressing you down, a pack filled with the hiking essentials Sophie had insisted we needed to have with us. Meanwhile, she was back in Seattle, warm and dry, thousands of miles away from the nearest midge. I lay there for a few minutes, cursing Sophie, the rain, the midges, and myself for being there in the first place.

As I struggled to my feet, I thought I saw movement in the stand of pines to my right. Of course, between the rain pounding my hat and my own ragged breathing, I wouldn't even have been able to hear a herd of wild sheep thundering by. I only had one sense to rely on. So, I stood there watching, waiting for something or someone to burst out from the greenery. But nothing happened. Were there deer in the area? Or something more dangerous, like bears? Or was my imagination working overtime?

Finally, I gave up waiting for something to emerge from the trees and started walking toward what, as I drew nearer, looked more and more like a body. Although I was still hoping it wasn't. For me as well as for the potential victim.

The rain suddenly let up and most of the midges vanished with it. I didn't question why; I just reveled in the reprieve as I approached the figure that had lured me to the bottom of the ravine. His eyes were open, but he wasn't blinking. His brown knit cap had a tear on the side with dark stains around the gap. If there had been more blood earlier, the rain had washed it away. He was wearing a green windbreaker, jeans and sneakers, his body twisted to one side with his right leg stuck out at an awkward angle. I had no doubt he was dead but forced myself to kneel down and check his neck for vitals.

His backpack was on the ground about five feet away. That struck me as an odd, but not impossible scenario. It could have fallen off toward the end of his descent, landing nearby. Maybe he had been taking something out of it when he fell, holding on until just before he slammed up against the boulder. The impact could have caused it to fly out of his hands. Or maybe an animal dragged it away.

I got up and went over to the charcoal grey backpack. It was damp but not damaged as far as I could see. The small compartment in front was partially unzipped. Kneeling down, I unzipped it the rest of the way and looked inside. There was a wallet and keys. I hesitated for a moment, wondering whether I should be going through his belongings. Then I decided it was more important to find out the identity of the backpack's owner than to worry about his privacy. I removed his driver's license and stared at the picture. It was a perfect match for the young man lying next to the boulder. I had found the body of Jared Blaine. Male, 5-11, 175 pounds, brown eyes. Then I noted his address.

He was from Seattle.

Amazing. What were the odds of finding the body of someone from your hometown on another continent?

There were a few business cards in the second slot in his wallet. I put his driver's license back and slipped one of the business cards out, then froze. My back was to the stand of trees. It was quiet now that the rain had stopped, and I thought I'd heard something. Just what, I wasn't sure. I waited a few seconds and didn't hear anything more. But something felt wrong. And I had a long time ago learned to act on instinct. I quickly put the wallet back in the pack and slipped the business card into my pocket. Then I got up and casually looked around before starting off in the direction of where the stream disappeared around the bend.

Trying not to appear as though I was running away, I didn't look back until I reached the cover of a stunted pine tree. Then I casually glanced over my shoulder, just a hiker checking where they had come from, not someone who feared they were being followed.

No humans or animals appeared to be stalking me. There was nothing between me and the body but an expanse of ground-hugging greenery. I felt foolish for getting spooked. But not so foolish that I'd changed my mind about continuing on. Jared Blaine would still be dead when I felt comfortable enough to stop and contact the authorities.

CHAPTER 2

disappearing act

The ground was uneven, studded with rocks and patches of dense undergrowth. My foot came down on a pointy rock at an awkward angle, and I almost fell. "Take it easy," I told myself. You've broken rules #1 and #2. No one knows where you are. So no one would come looking if I injured myself and couldn't call for help. And if there *was* some person or some animal following me, I *definitely* didn't want to become incapacitated.

When I reached the point where the stream took a sharp turn and disappeared from sight, I slowed down and asked myself if I was being stupid to run away from a shadow and an indistinct sound. As I saw it, I had two choices: I could ignore my intuition and go back and stay with the body while waiting for the authorities, or I could continue on and make my call once I managed to find my way back up to the trail.

Still unable to shake the feeling I wasn't alone in the ravine, I opted for door number two. But first I decided to do a reality check.

There were some large rocks and a small cluster of trees a short distance ahead. When I reached them, instead of continuing to the left, I ducked behind the rocks and quickly moved to the last one. It had started to rain again, not a heavy rain but a persistent, unpleasant drizzle. I knelt down and peeked around the rock, barely breathing, watching for any sign of movement. I stayed there for what seemed like hours, but it was more likely about five minutes. Waiting and watching. Watching and waiting. Holding my breath until I had to breathe, even though there was no one to hear me.

The maneuver was all for nothing. I saw no people. No animals. Nothing. Even the midges had deserted me.

Although the facts seemed to bear out that I wasn't being followed, I still didn't feel like retracing my steps. Once you get spooked by something it's hard to get it out of your head. Maybe if it had been a sunny day or if Sophie had been with me . . . damn, this was *her* fault. She was the one who had picked this area to hike in. I was just there to show her what she was missing and to make her sorry she had bailed. Of course, if I wanted to succeed at that, I would have to leave out references to the rain and the midges. And now, to the body.

Eventually the steep hillside gave way to a more gentle slope, and I found a fairly easy place to work my way back up to the trail. When I stepped onto the dirt path, I was so relieved to be out of the brush that I didn't even complain when the midges returned to taunt me. Well, not out loud, that is.

At that point I texted the Mountain Rescue Team number to let them know I had found the body of a hiker, which trail I was on, and that I was headed back to the car park. It didn't take long before I had a return text telling me a team would leave immediately and that they would either meet me in the car park or on the trail. I knew I would have to go back to show them where the body was, but at least I wouldn't have to descend that hillside again. And I would no longer be alone.

I estimated that I was almost back to the car park when I saw the three figures headed toward me on the trail. Two men and a woman, all in different colored raingear and rain hats, all wearing heavy looking packs. One of the men had a coil of rope over his shoulder. The other was using walking sticks. I've always considered walking sticks an affectation and was surprised to see someone from a rescue team using them.

As they got closer there was one thing that really stood—they weren't encircled by midges! Did the beasties like foreign food or was there some secret formula for keeping them at bay? It seemed self-centered to focus on my discomfort while these volunteers had come to retrieve a body, but I promised myself that before we parted company, I would find out how they did it.

"You Bryn?" the taller of the two men asked as they drew near. He was wearing a bright red jacket with his hood cinched in around his face.

"Yes," I said. "Glad you could make it so quickly."

"You indicated that the person was deceased," he said.

"He *is*." But I was still glad they hadn't wasted any time responding. The sooner I got out of there the better.

"I'm Allen," the tall man said, "and this is Campbell . . ."

Campbell nodded and smiled. He was wearing a yellow raincoat, but he hadn't bothered to put up his hood. His light brown hair glistened with rainwater.

"And I'm Fiona," the young woman said.

Of course, you are, I thought. She was the perfect Scottish, outdoors sort with strawberry blond hair, pink cheeks and delicate features that didn't match her obvious athleticism. I instantly liked and envied her.

"How far away is the body?" Campbell asked.

"I'm not sure. I came back along the floor of the ravine, and that took more time than if I'd been on the trail. My guess is it's another quarter of an hour or so up to the place where I climbed down to take a look."

"Are you alone?" Fiona asked.

"Yes." I almost expected a lecture on why it wasn't safe to hike in the area on your own, but none came.

"Well, let's get going," Allen said, motioning for me to take the lead.

The rain had started again in earnest. I was tired, miserable, and hungry. With all of the midges hovering in my face I hadn't bothered to try to eat anything. How I longed to turn around and head to the inn where I was staying instead of trudging back up that damn hill.

Fiona came up behind me and asked, "Where are you from?"

"United States, West Coast," I said, not feeling chatty, although appreciating her attempt at conversation.

"I went to New York once," she said. "Loved it. But I've never been on the West Coast. Heard it rains a lot there." Was she being funny?

"No midges though," I said pointedly.

"Oh." She seemed to notice my problem for the first time.

"They like you, huh?"

"Seem to."

"What are you using?"

"DEET."

"That's bad stuff. You should try Avon Skin So Soft."

"Is that what you use?" Without even half trying, I was getting an answer to my question.

"No, I don't use anything. They just don't like me."

"Is it your politics or your religion?"

It took her a moment before she realized I was kidding. "No, I like to think I live right." I could hear the smile in her voice.

"Really?" *Really!*

"Oh, I didn't mean it like that. No one knows why they stay away from some people and go after others. But a swarm can inflict about 3,000 bites in an hour, so you need to wear protection if you're a person they're attracted to."

"There are things I would rather attract." I started feeling sorry for myself again.

"Well, this area is particularly bad for midges. It should get better—unless you are planning on hiking a lot in the Highlands."

"I *was*, but I doubt I will now."

"I can give you some suggestions about where you might want to go instead, if you're interested."

That was an offer I was definitely going to take her up on. There was absolutely no reason, other than stubbornness, that I had to stick to Sophie's itinerary.

We all hiked in silence for a while. Well, silence except for the pounding rain and my heavy breathing. All the hiking and stress was really starting to get to me. But since I was in the lead, and since I wanted to get this over with as quickly as possible, I tried to maintain a brisk pace. Brisk for me, probably snail slow for them. My guess was that was why they had me in the lead. So I could control how fast we walked based on my capabilities. Even so, by the time we got back to where it had all begun, I was exhausted.

"Here," I said stopping. I pointed at the boulder in the ravine. Then I blinked hard. 'I'm sure this is the spot . . .," I began, looking around. "I'm positive. He was right down there, up against that boulder." *Was*—that was the operative word. There appeared to be nothing down there now but brush and rock.

Campbell and Allen exchanged looks. Fiona turned to me and said, "Take your time. It's easy to get confused in these hills. There's not much variety in the scenery."

If it hadn't been raining so hard, I was sure they would have seen my footprints at the edge of the trail. But any indication that I had once stood there looking down at the boulder below had been completely washed away. Was it too late to mention that I'd been spooked by someone or something in the ravine? Or, since I hadn't brought it up before, would that just make me seem even less credible?

I peered over the edge and scanned the area. There was no sign of either the body or the pack. Had some animal dragged the body off into the bush? Then come back and dragged the pack off? That didn't seem likely. It had to have been a person who moved the body and taken the pack. But why?

"Are you certain he was dead?" Campbell asked. "Maybe he came to and hiked out."

The question put me on the defensive, but I tried to keep my tone neutral. "I'm sure, and besides, he had what looked to be a broken leg. Even if he was still alive, he wasn't walking anywhere on his own."

"Maybe he had some friends in the area that you didn't see," Campbell suggested, although he didn't sound like that's what he thought had happened.

My mind was racing, searching for logical answers. Where was Jared Blaine? Why wasn't his body lying down there next to the boulder? Given that I had sensed another presence when checking out the body, was it possible Blaine's fall hadn't been an accident? But even if it had been a deliberate act, even if he had been shoved over the edge and had fallen to his death, why move the body?

"Should we go a bit further up the trail?" Allen asked with a touch of impatience in his voice.

"I was right here," I said, calmly and firmly. "I remember how I traversed the hillside . . . and where I came out below." I pointed to the route I had taken. "And the trees to the right, and the bend in the creek to the left." Again pointing.

"Well, we could go down and take a look," Fiona offered.

"That's a long way down for no reason," Allen said.

"I don't' know what to say . . .," I began, but I really didn't know what to say, so I let my sentence trail off into the rain.

"Come on, Fiona," Campbell said. "You and I can go down there and have a look around. It won't take that long." Allen obviously didn't want them to go, but finally nodded in agreement. Fiona and Campbell started down, displaying a lot more agility than I had exhibited earlier, Campbell using his sticks to steady himself. It crossed my mind that it would have made my descent easier if I'd had a pair of walking sticks.

As we watched them make their way down the slope, Allen's irritation was as thick as the swarm of midges that continued dogging me.

"I'm sorry," I said. "I don't understand what happened to Jared Blaine's body."

Allen turned toward me. "You know his name? Were you with him?" He sounded more irritated than surprised.

"No, I wasn't with him. I looked in his wallet."

"You searched him for his wallet?" Now he not only sounded irritated, but suspicious.

"No, it was in his pack," I explained. "The small outside pocket was unzipped, so I looked inside."

"Do you have the wallet?"

"No, I put it back in the pack." I didn't know what he was getting at, but I didn't like his tone. And I was reluctant to explain why I'd dropped everything and left in a hurry. "Look, it may not have been logical, but I had just come across a dead man. I wasn't thinking too clearly."

He glanced down at his two colleagues. They were almost at the boulder. "You're absolutely sure this is the right place?"

In my mind it was possible to be rattled and clear-headed at the same time, but Allen's tone suggested that he thought I was either mistaken about the location or delusional. And I feared he was leaning toward the latter. My only hope was that Fiona and Campbell would find something to suggest there had been a body there earlier.

We watched as they looked carefully at the boulder and searched the surrounding area. Finally, they looked up at us and shook their heads. They hadn't found anything.

"I know what I saw," I said stubbornly.

"Well, we gave it a try. I'm not sure what else we can do."

His dismissive attitude made me even more defensive. It seemed to me there must be something *they* or *we* or *I* could do. If we just gave it some thought. I considered telling him where Jared Blaine was from, but if he turned up missing, that would come out soon enough. And somehow the fact that I hadn't mentioned it initially made me seem more like a suspect than someone who just happened to be in the right or wrong place at the right or wrong time. Depending on how you looked at it. So I kept my mouth shut.

By the time Fiona and Campbell rejoined us on the trail, the atmosphere was charged with annoyance, disbelief, and, around me at least, midges. It was clear that Allen was convinced we were either in the wrong place or that the "body" had come to life and left the area under its own steam. And Fiona and Campbell seemed inclined to agree. As for me, I was tired and discouraged, almost relieved to give up the search and head back to the car park. But in my mind, I kept going over and over what had happened, how the body had disappeared, and asking myself whether I should have done something different.

CHAPTER 3

a call from the grave

When we got back to the car park, I apologized for calling them out on a wild goose chase, even though I didn't believe I had. Allen waved my apology away and left without saying anything. Campbell told me not to feel bad, not finding a body was *good* news. And Fiona asked if I wanted to meet her for drinks later. We agreed on a time and place and, with my team of midges in tow, I headed for my car.

As I clicked the locks on my rental car it suddenly occurred to me that the midges could and would follow me inside when I opened the door. Then I would be trapped inside with the horde. And if I took off my rain jacket, I would have even more skin exposed.

I stood there staring at the door, desperately trying to come up with a plan. But my mind was blank.

"Need some help?" a male voice asked in that lovely brogue that is to me quintessential Scotland. I'd read that accents varied by region in Scotland, just like in the United States, but to my untrained ear all brogues sounded alike. And deliciously sexy.

I turned toward the man offering to rescue the maiden in distress and was immediately consumed by deep ocean blue eyes and a smile to melt the hardest heart.

15

"Only if you can make these midges disappear."

"Can do," he said with confidence.

At first, I thought he was kidding. He took out a pack of cigarettes, lit one and began blowing smoke on *my* midges. They had been hanging around me so long I was beginning to think of them as "mine." As the smoke replaced the midges, I could hardly believe my eyes. And as much as I dislike the smell of cigarette smoke normally, at that moment it was as welcome as the first whiff of freshly ground coffee in the morning.

"You'd better get in quick. They might return."

"I can't tell you how grateful I am . . ."

"You could show me by letting me buy you a drink later," he said. "Where are you staying?"

Too overwhelmed to think through what was happening, I told him my name and where I was staying. He said he'd call, blew some more smoke at me, and helped me slip inside without a single midge in pursuit. I waved at him through the window, feeling both flattered by his attention and a bit foolish. But I'd been through a lot in the last few hours and felt I deserved a moment of romantic fantasy.

Back at the inn I quickly stripped off my clothes and got into the shower. As tired as I was, I also felt violated by the weather, the bugs and the DEET.

I was bent over the controls on the tub, twisting knobs while trying to interpret the markings on them when icy water found its way through the showerhead and spit on the back of my neck. I leapt back and moved the handle to what I hoped was "hot." Then I fiddled with the controls some more to increase the water pressure. I finally had to settle for lukewarm and barely animated. But with soap and determination I washed away the detritus of the day, wrapped myself in a harsh white towel, and collapsed in a very uncomfortable chair. Not quite the ending I'd been hoping for, but at least I wasn't still on that steep hillside with vines waiting to lasso my feet. Or lying at the bottom of the ravine next to a boulder. Like poor disappearing and very dead Jared Blaine from my hometown.

Finally, motivated by hunger and thirst, I got up and tried to brush some of the tangles out of my long red, straight hair. Straight hair and almost six feet tall, the bane of my existence when I was younger. Now it doesn't seem to matter. I have good skin that doesn't require make-up, and I'm not bad looking, just not your TV personality beauty.

As soon as I was presentable, I headed downstairs for something to eat. Admittedly I suffer from an irrational fear of haggis, a childhood dislike of game meat, and an aversion to the unsavory ingredients in black pudding. But fortunately, Sophie's choice of places to stay in the area had not been driven by the desire for traditional cuisine. The menu offered a wide variety of local options. I ordered fried haddock with pea and potato mash and studied the dessert menu while waiting for my meal to arrive.

There were quite a few fellow diners in the room, but so far, my experience with meeting people while traveling alone hadn't been all that great. With the exception of the encounter with the devilishly handsome, blue-eyed Scot in the parking lot. Which, in retrospect, seemed odd. Although I had undoubtedly looked needy. Needy, but not exactly date material in my saturated rain gear surrounded by midges. Oh well, a chance encounter that would probably go nowhere but would at least be one pleasant memory moment from an otherwise miserable day. When my plate of food was set before me, I didn't hesitate. In no time at all I had inhaled the entire offering and was contemplating scooping up the remaining potato glop with my finger when a male voice said: "I like a woman who enjoys her food."

I looked up and found myself staring into those same blue eyes from the car park. "Hope you don't mind if I join you," he said as he pulled out a chair and sat down. I couldn't imagine that many women asked him to make himself scarce. He was tall, muscular, and irresistibly appealing in an outdoorsy, ski bum sort of way. The dimple on his chin was a bonus.

"Please do," I said, after staring a moment too long before saying anything. "I wasn't expecting you." I couldn't believe I had said something so mundane. What happened to all those clever comebacks I'd seen in the romantic comedies Sophie insists we watch?

"I was in the neighborhood, so I thought it might be easier to drop by rather than call." Of course, with his accent what he said sounded like a caress rather than an explanation. "Ready for that drink? We could go to one of the bars here or to a nearby pub." He laughed. "In Scotland there's always a pub nearby."

I glanced at my watch. "I'm meeting a friend in the lounge in about an hour," I said with a touch of regret.

"Then why don't we go there? You can get a jumpstart on him . . . her?"

"She's a 'her,'" I said, mentally kicking myself for sounding like an eager schoolgirl being approached by the captain of the football team. Still, I didn't protest as he stood and helped me out of my chair. I was on vacation. I could indulge in a flirtation or fling if I wanted. And since I was on my own, no one would have to know if I said or did something stupid. The story would be mine to tell any way I wanted to tell it.

In the hour before Fiona arrived, I had a very pale, golden beer made with heather from the Highland moorlands that tasted just like what I imaged liquid heather would taste like. While I drank, I poured my heart out about my terrible day. Keith was a fantastic listener. He smiled and nodded in all the right places and was sufficiently empathetic to buoy my spirits considerably. Just sitting across from such a good-looking man was a morale booster. Yet, for some reason I wasn't completely honest with him. I didn't tell him how certain I had been that the man was dead. Nor did I tell him about going through the guy's wallet. Instead, I'd emphasized my difficulty with the descent and gave him Allen's version about the hiker probably not being as badly injured as I'd thought at first. "Although," I admitted, "I have trouble imagining that he simply got up and hightailed it out of there when I went for help."

"Well, it's not impossible. He might have been confused and wandered off in the other direction," Keith said.

"Yes, that's probably what happened," I agreed. "And that's what the rescue team concluded."

"You didn't recognize him, did you?" Keith asked.

"No. I've only been in Scotland a few days, and I didn't meet any other hikers on the trail."

"So, the mystery hiker will remain a mystery," Keith said as he finished off his drink.

Fiona suddenly appeared, looked from me to Keith and back. "Private party?" she asked.

"No," I said. "Keith was keeping me company until you arrived."

"Yes," Keith said. "I was just leaving." As he stood up and yielded his seat to Fiona, he turned to me and said, "Enjoy the rest of your trip."

"I will," I said, somewhat surprised he was leaving so abruptly. I'd expected him to suggest we get together again, maybe ask me to delay my departure from the area or offer to meet me somewhere down the line. So much for a fling with an attractive Scotsman.

The waiter came over and took Fiona's drink order. Then she looked me in the eye and asked, "So what were you doing with bad-boy Keith?"

"Bad-boy?"

"Maybe I should ask how well you know him before I say more."

"Not at all. I met him in the car park earlier. Then he showed up here about an hour ago."

"What did he want?" she asked. Then, blushing, she quickly added, "I mean, it's none of my business. It's just—"

"Is there something about him that I should know?"

"It depends."

"Well, I don't expect to see him again. You heard him tell me to enjoy the rest of my trip. So 'fess up.'"

"It's just that he's, well . . . to put it bluntly, he's quite the womanizer and has some dubious family connections. Not that he's ever been convicted of anything. Not that I know of, at least. But he uses people."

"He does have the charm of a con man," I admitted.

"And the looks of a . . ."

". . . real hottie," I finished for her.

She laughed. "Those eyes."

"And that dimple."

"And those abs."

We both laughed. "I admit I was hoping for a bit more than a drink, but that's the way it goes."

"Maybe I scared him off. Sorry."

"I should probably thank you. I've had enough trouble on this trip so far. Seriously, I was surprised when he came by. But it didn't feel like there was any agenda during our conversation."

"Did you tell him about finding a body?"

It was my turn to blush. "Well, yes and no. I didn't want to sound like an idiot, so I told him the story Allen suggested—that I came across what I thought was a body at the bottom of the ravine, but the guy wasn't there when I came back with help, so he had obviously come to and walked away on his own." I paused briefly, then added, "I do, however, realize that what Allen actually thinks is that I'm totally out of it and either didn't see anything or that it happened at a different place further up the trail."

"What do *you* really think happened?" Fiona asked, suddenly very serious.

"I know what I saw, but I can't come up with anything to explain why someone would move a body under those circumstances."

"But that's what you think, isn't it, that someone moved the body?"

I took a deep breath. "I don't know. It all seems like a bad dream now. And it probably doesn't matter what I think. There was no body. End of story. And tomorrow I'm going somewhere without midges, somewhere a fair distance from here."

Fiona smiled. "And that's why I'm here. After the day you've had, and having to put up with Allen's rudeness, I want to help you find something a little more satisfying for the next leg of your journey." She pulled a map out of her purse and spread it out between us on the table. A half hour later I had a new plan. One that sounded both interesting and fun. No more midges. No more rain. And, preferably, no more bodies.

We stayed another hour chatting about our lives and the differences between our two countries. I liked her and her perspectives. If we'd lived closer to each other we might have become friends. As it was, I promised to text her to let her know how the rest of my trip went. And she promised to let me know if the body was discovered a second time. But even I didn't think that was going to happen.

The next morning, I got up early, made some travel arrangements, took another unsatisfactory shower and packed my suitcase. Although I was looking forward to moving on, I had tossed and turned all night worrying about what had happened and whether there was something I could or should do to follow up.

There were several brochures on the narrow table in front of the tiny window in my room. One in particular caught my eye. It not only listed local attractions but places to stay in and near the small village. It occurred to me that one thing I could do was to call around to see if I could locate where Jared Blaine had been or *was* staying. Maybe he would surprise me by answering his phone. It was a little like hoping to see Santa

Claus eating the cookies you'd left out for him when you were five years old. But on the other hand, I would be happy—if shocked—to find him alive.

There were eight accommodations listed on the brochure. I started with the easiest, the reception desk at the inn where I was staying. I told the clerk I was trying to get in touch with Jared Blaine and had forgotten which room he was in. To my surprise, I scored with my first call; he was staying in the same place I was. And, since I was a fellow guest, the clerk didn't hesitate to tell me his room number. "Could you put me through, please?" I asked, my heart starting to pound.

"Sorry, but I have a note here saying that Mr. Blaine called late yesterday to let us know he's taking a side trip and won't be returning until the end of the week at the earliest. We're holding his room for him."

It took a few seconds for what she had said to sink in. Then I thanked her for the information and hung up. For a while I sat there staring at the phone, trying to decide whether she'd been wrong about the timing or whether I was losing my mind. Finally, I came to the conclusion that there was at least one other possibility—someone else had called to keep the inn from reporting Blaine's disappearance. Not a happy thought.

So, what was I going to do? Without a body and with the staff at the inn believing Blaine had taken a side trip and would return later in the week, no one would be looking for him any time soon. And I was more than ready to leave the area and the midges behind. At the same time, I couldn't just walk away with so many unanswered questions.

Ten minutes later I was standing in front of Blaine's room. The inn had been updated in many ways, but it still had old-fashion key locks. Using a credit card and several muttered swear words, I managed to manipulate the latch between the door and the frame. Moments later I was inside.

The room was very similar to mine, small and sparsely furnished, with a bed dominating the main room. Blaine's suitcase was open on the bed, clothes spilled out like he had left in a hurry. Or . . . like someone had conducted a quick search of its contents. If so, I probably wasn't going to find anything helpful. But I had to look.

There didn't seem to be anything special about his clothes.

Just what you'd expect to see for someone on holiday in Scotland. I checked pockets. Nothing. I felt around the lining of the suitcase for bulges. Nothing. But I did notice one strange thing—the designer luggage tag on his suitcase was empty. Why have a fancy tag if you don't put your name and address in it?

The lack of identification on the tag made me curious. I searched the rest of the room looking for something with Blaine's name on it. There didn't appear to be a single thing to identify the room's occupant. How curious. Had Blaine taken all of his identification with him on a hike? If not, why would anyone remove all of his personal information? He was registered at the inn. Under the name on his driver's license. And he probably used a credit card to secure his reservation. So it wouldn't take much to trace him. Although the absence of information might slow things down a bit. But, even so, why would anyone want to keep Jared Blaine's death a secret for such a short period of time? It seemed like a lot of work for very little gain.

I was just about to leave when there was a knock on the door. "Room service," a female voice called. My heart started racing. Shit. Why hadn't I put out the "do not disturb" sign? At this point my options seemed limited, but I had to do something, and fast.

The only thing I could think of was to hide behind the door. Maybe I would get an opportunity to slip out once she came in to do the cleaning. Did they leave the door open when they were cleaning a room? I didn't know. One way or the other I would either manage to get away, or I would get caught. Maybe I could claim to be Jared's girlfriend. Maybe I should have jumped in the bed rather than hiding behind the door. Too late; I was committed.

I heard her put the key in the lock . . . then . . . nothing. No one turned the handle and opened the door. Had she changed her mind? Had she heard me and suspected something? Was she hurrying off to notify security? Or had it been someone other than a hotel employee on the other side of the door?

There didn't seem to be any option but to open the door and take a look. I slowly turned the handle, paused to listen, then opened the door a crack. There was no one standing right outside, just a cart with cleaning supplies. I opened the door a few inches more and peeked through the narrow space down the hall. No one in sight. Moving as fast and as silently as I could, I quickly stepped into the hall, softly closing the door behind me, and then tried to look casual as I headed toward the stairs.

The maid came out of a small room carrying some toilet paper just as I passed by. Apparently, she'd forgotten to load her cart properly before letting herself in to clean. Kismet? A lucky break? A one-time pass on bad luck? Unless they had hidden cameras somewhere that I hadn't noticed, I was hopefully in the clear.

Once back in my room I agonized over what to do next. I didn't actually have any facts. It was all conjecture, conjecture founded on the belief that Jaren Blaine had died in that ravine.

Without the body or some kind of evidence, I didn't see what I could do.

After considerable soul searching, I texted Fiona and said I was leaving shortly but would like to talk for a few minutes. When she returned my call, I told her that the missing hiker was staying at the inn and had called to let them know he wouldn't be back until the end of the week. I suggested she might want to follow through then. There was an awkward pause before she said, "Allen may have been right."

Out loud I agreed, but in my heart, I knew the call had been made by a voice from the grave.

CHAPTER 4

quidbye scotland

I had spent the first night of my vacation at a lovely hotel in Kirkbean by Dumfries, a place Sophie had chosen for its history and ambiance. Built in 1752 by a tobacco baron, it was the perfect movie set for a period drama with extensive, well-groomed grounds, quaint rooms furnished with antiques, and an atmosphere of gentility and wealth. Just as promised, the food had been outstanding. But for some reason it had made me feel like a displaced Jane Eyre.

Next, thanks to Sophie's decision that we should hike in the Highlands, I'd experienced the rain and the midges.

Today I had a plan of my own, and I was determined to enjoy the rest of my vacation.

I spent most of what was left of the day driving up the Great Glen, stopping several times to look for Nessie. Although I was still in midge country, they were either taking a break or plaguing some other poor devil. By the time I reached Inverness I was ready for the bustle of city life. Fiona had recommended a picturesque B&B along the banks of the River Ness within a few minutes' walk of downtown. The owners were warm and welcoming. They suggested several places for dinner, and after an excellent meal and a pleasant, bug-free stroll, I gratefully sank into a comfortable bed and immediately fell asleep.

One restful night and far too much breakfast later, I toured Inverness with its castles, historic buildings, old churches, and museums. It was a typical tourist day, no challenging terrain, no bugs, no downpours, and, most important, no bodies. But even as I was enjoying myself, I kept going over and over the events of the other day, speculating on possible scenarios, wondering if I would ever know what had happened.

The next day I drove to a small village that was billed as one of the "driest and sunniest places in the whole of Scotland." Fiona had assured me there were plenty of interesting places nearby to walk and sightsee. Once again, she had recommended a B&B, one that boasted its resident dog had been crowned "the scruffiest dog in Scotland," an interesting if dubious distinction. I was immediately taken with the charm of the B&B, its hosts, and its very scruffy but loveable dog, Dudley. I took several pictures of myself with Dudley and sent them back to some friends, including Sophie. I didn't, however, explain to her why I was fraternizing with Dudley rather than hiking in the Highlands. There would be time enough for that later.

I spent the rest of my vacation doing more sightseeing than hiking. Each place I stopped I pored over the local lists of things to see and do. I visited churches, castles, museums, and markets— then more castles and churches. I walked on beaches, hiked in planned forests, and explored windswept stretches of land, of glens and dunes. I also checked out more than my share of pubs. That was one thing Keith had been right on about—there were pubs everywhere, even in the smallest of villages.

Pubs and castles. After two weeks I'd had my fill of both.

It was almost with a feeling of relief that I dropped off my car and got on a shuttle to the airport. I had promised myself that I wouldn't text Fiona until I was about to leave, but each day I had been tempted to break my resolve. With two hours before my flight was scheduled to take off, I finally succumbed. It only took her about ten minutes to respond. According to the inn staff, Blaine had called a second time to ask them to pack up his things and hold onto them for at least another week. And he'd sent them a cashier's check to cover his bill. "Nothing more I can do," she texted.

Nothing more I could do either. At least not while in Scotland.

there's no one like macavity

It was midnight by the time I got home to the Lake Union marina where I live aboard my 40-foot sailboat, the *Aspara*. I was so tired I could barely walk. And it was raining. A fitting end to my vacation. My wheeled suitcase echoed eerily as I rolled it down the wood dock and out onto the old cement pier where my boat was moored.

I flipped back the blue plastic tarp that covered the aft deck and climbed into the cockpit. Even with the light at the end of the dock I could barely see to unlock the padlock on my hatch. I didn't bother taking out the door slats; I just stepped over them and hauled my suitcase in after me. Then I slid the hatch back, secured the deadbolt, stripped off what I was wearing, and tossed everything on the settee. After that I immediately headed for my bunk.

There was no transition from being asleep to being awake. The sound of a very irate cat howling up a storm abruptly filled my consciousness. It took me a moment to register the fact that I hadn't opened the porthole my cat uses as a cat door. Technically my neighbor, Logan, was still cat sitting but apparently my demanding pet didn't realize that.

"Dammit, Macavity, can't you let me sleep in just this once?" I yelled. And how did he know I was there? Then again, maybe he didn't. Maybe this had been his morning ritual since I had gone on vacation. Throw a fit on the back deck and wake up anyone staying on their boat in the marina.

I dragged myself out of my bunk, pulled on a robe and went into the main cabin to let in my large orange cat and stop the commotion.

As soon as I pulled back the hatch Macavity leapt down the steps and went over to his food bowl. Then he glared up at me as if I'd left him on his own without anything to eat for two and a half weeks.

"You don't look like you've lost any weight," I said as I got out a can of his favorite, Fancy Feast Salmon and Shrimp. I normally reserve that for special occasions, but it was handy, and I wanted to keep the peace. "Hasn't Logan been feeding you?" I asked as I pried up the tab on the top of the can. As if on cue, Logan yelled,

"Bryn, you up?"

The next thing I knew he was peering down at me from the aft deck.

"Can't someone have a little privacy around here?"

"Sorry," he said not sounding at all sorry. "I thought you might stop by last night when you got in." Logan and his partner, Judd, live one dock over on their 53-foot ferro cement sailboat, the *Carpe Diem*.

"It was late, and I was tired."

"You look pretty rugged," he observed.

"Macavity woke me up. I haven't even had a chance to . . .

do anything." I hate the word "pee," but that's what I needed to do.

Macavity was butting his head against my legs, urging me to get on with serving him his breakfast. "Want me to come back later?" Logan asked.

"You're clairvoyant," I said a bit testily. "Give me a half hour, okay?"

"How about some breakfast at Beth's?" Beth's was a small cafe across from the marina. It's sandwiched between a handful of marine-related businesses and several small start-ups with unrecognizable names that gravitate to the run-down, low-rent buildings on the dead-end street. There are a number of other cafes and delis within walking distance that serve healthier options from menus not worn and stained with years of use, but we prefer Beth's.

"It's a deal. I'll come get you when I'm ready."

<hr>

Logan is one of the few people I am completely honest with, about everything—my feelings, insecurities, dreams—and I also share the daily ups and downs of life with him. Sophie is my long-time best friend, but Logan is my red-haired soul mate. His partner, Judd, is an uptight lawyer who I respect and like, but we will never be close. For one thing he doesn't like cats. Or he *says* he doesn't like cats. He and Macavity have developed a relationship of sorts. Maybe Macavity would have been a lawyer if he'd been human.

So, when Logan and I hooked up to go to breakfast and he asked about my vacation, I didn't hold back. I told him about my initial determination to make Sophie regret she hadn't come with me and how quickly that resolve had vanished after the first real day of hiking.

By the time we had our breakfasts ordered and were seated, I was to the part about discovering the body of Jared Blaine. "A local guy, huh? What a coincidence."

"Yes, and as near as I could tell, he was hiking by himself, like me."

"And you have his card?"

"Yes, in my suitcase. I haven't unpacked yet. But it said he worked for Humanity Health Group. HHG. Strange name. I've googled them, of course, but they don't seem to have much of a web presence."

"Oh, I know about them."

"You do?"

"Don't you remember when NorPac Medical Group had all of those protesters and one of their buildings was torched?"

"Sure, I remember that. It was pretty ugly. But I don't remember the details. Something about biomedicine, wasn't it?"

"Yeah, it was over what is called chimera research. Fascinating stuff. Humanity Health Group is a division of NorPac that is working on growing human organs by implanting stem cells into the embryos of pigs and sheep."

"It's coming back . . . It made the news. A bunch of people picketed the place and shouted insults at the employees."

"Yeah. The research was funded by the government for a while, until the public started raising hell," Logan said. "Apparently there is some issue about whether human cells introduced into animals will go where intended. Scientists argue they can track what's happening and will stop any experiment if it looks as though something isn't proceeding as planned. But the question is what happens if they don't stop the process in time. For example, what if they're trying to create a pancreas and some human cells find their way to a sheep's brain? Instead of a harvestable pancreas you'd end up with a smart sheep. Opponents claim it could blur the line between species."

"So, if you're a scientist in biomedicine, you think of this as a potential medical breakthrough that can benefit humanity. But if you're fixated on the potential for unforeseen consequences, you start envisioning pigs playing chess and sheep running for Congress. And maybe you panic."

Amy, our server, put a plate of bacon and eggs in front of me. I thanked her, took a few bites while considering the ethics of biomedical research. "Sounds complicated," I concluded. "I'm not sure how I feel about it."

"Me neither. But in Greek mythology the chimera was a bad omen."

"Well, I can imagine there's a lot of room for error in that kind of research."

"And, of course, some people don't like the use of animals for medical experiments of any kind."

"I have mixed feelings about that, too. But if I had to choose between you and a sheep . . . well, let me think about that a minute."

Logan pretended to lob some hash browns at me, and I pretended to duck.

"Seriously," I said, "I know there have been instances of animals abused in the name of medical research. But if that's the only way we can get the knowledge needed to save human lives, well . . . it seems to me that we should be talking about how the animals are treated, not doing away with the research altogether."

"But what *if* some pig or rat or whatever animal they use for an experiment acquires some human characteristics such as the ability to speak. Then what?" Logan said.

"Sounds kinda science *fictiony* to me."

"But not impossible under the right—or the wrong—circumstances."

"So . . . what if Jared was one of the bad guys, someone taking chances with his research. Or being cruel to his animal subjects. Do you think someone would follow him all the way to Scotland and push him over a cliff?" I was beginning to think it was a possibility.

"Doesn't sound too likely, does it?"

"No, it doesn't. And if someone did him in, why hide the body and call the inn to say he would eventually come by and pick up his things? Surely someone is going to report him missing; that ruse only works for so long."

We concentrated on our breakfasts for a few minutes. Then Logan asked, "What are you going to do?"

"What makes you think I'm going to do anything?"

"Come on, Bryn. It's me, Logan. What are you going to do?"

"Okay, you're right. I can't just put it behind me and go on as if nothing happened. I was thinking of dropping by Humanity Health Group to see if he's back from vacation yet. See what they have to say."

"Want company?"

"No classes today?"

"The University is being kind to me. I'm on a Monday-Wednesday-Friday schedule this quarter."

"Must be nice."

"This from the consultant who sets her own hours."

"*When* I can get work. At least you have a steady income."

"Yeah, in another ten years I'll be able to pay off my student loans."

"Don't give me that crap.

"Okay, so I owe my parents instead of the government. But some days I think it might have been better to owe the government."

"Come on, your parents are great."

"Just because they like you doesn't give you the right to defend them."

Logan was partly kidding, partly serious. His parents were wealthy and often tried to use their position and money to try to influence his lifestyle. But they stopped just short of pushing so hard that they drove him away.

I wanted to unpack and check my email before heading over to Humanity Health Group, so we agreed to meet at 1:00. Macavity met me halfway down the dock, circling around my legs like a hostile predator, letting me know just how mad he was that I had abandoned him for so long.

"Get over it," I said, and Macavity glared up at me with his one green eye and his one hazel eye. I glared back at him with my own mismatched eyes, but he always wins. His eyes were the reason I'd rescued him when he was only a kitten. I'd gone with a friend to get a cat for her and ended up with one of my own.

"Okay, I promise, I'll make it up to you."

Somewhat appeased, Macavity ran on ahead. I knew exactly where he'd be—standing next to his treat jar, expecting his usual and then some. Sometimes he can be a real pain. But I can't imagine life without him.

visitors not welcome

NorPac was on the east side of Lake Washington in an industrial park that looked more like a real park than an industrial area. There were lots of tall trees and winding paths and reed-lined ponds. The grounds around the buildings were nicely manicured and there appeared to be an emphasis on local vegetation. The road wove between rows of rhododendrons and around a series of older looking wood buildings, most of them no more than two or three stories, tucked into the vegetation like they were supposed to be vacation getaways rather than places where serious work took place.

There had been no address on Jared's card and no website for Humanity Health Group. The NorPac website didn't mention it either. Logan and I decided they were trying to avoid calling attention to this aspect of their business.

NorPac didn't advertise its existence in the industrial park to the average passer-by either. There was a sign, but it was small and far enough back from the main road that you almost had to know it was there in order to see it. Once we figured out which building belonged to NorPac, we parked in the area designated for visitors and walked up to the front door, only to realize it was a secure building. No code or escort, no entry.

"Now what?" Logan asked.

"Maybe someone will come out and we can sneak in."

"Or maybe we should try something more direct." He took out his cell phone, fiddled with it for a minute or so, then dialed a number. In a confident voice, he said, "Hi, we're friends of Jared Blaine and stopped by to see if we could catch up with him, but he isn't answering his phone." Pause.

"No, we didn't tell him we were coming. In fact, that's why we're here. We haven't heard from him since he came back from vacation. And we're starting to worry." Pause.

"My name is Logan Douglas, and Bryn Baczek is with me. We're at the front door. Any chance we can come in and talk to you about this?" Pause.

"Okay. Thanks."

Moments later a young woman peered at us through the glass door. She was wearing business casual, but her skirt was on the short side, as was the silk shell under her jacket. You could catch glimpses of a strip of flesh between her skirt and shell when she moved. I tried to look non-threatening and friendly. Logan always looks that way. After a few moments she opened the door. "You can't come in without an escort," she explained, blocking our entrance. It didn't sound like there were options, but she *had* opened the door.

"We just want to know if Jared's okay. He doesn't answer his phone, and we've left several messages." Logan was boldly winging it. "It isn't like him not to respond. Especially since we're supposed to get together next weekend for an overnight camping trip." He waited, looking boyishly appealing. She looked from him to me and seemed to be wavering.

"Maybe we could talk to Bill," Jared said. "He around?" Bill? Where had that come from?

"Bill Masters?"

"Yes, if we could ask him if he's heard from Jared . . ." He left the request hanging. We didn't want much, just reassurance that a friend was okay.

She hesitated, glancing around as if worried someone would see her talking to us. "You won't be able to get into the lab, but I'll let Bill know you're coming. He can meet you outside."

"Where?" Logan asked.

"It's the second building along the path." She pointed. "It was nice meeting you." She quickly disappeared inside, and the door snapped shut with a decisive click.

"It was nice meeting you, too," I said to the closed door. Logan raised his eyebrows and shrugged. "So," I said as we head down the path. "You were good. I think asking for Bill did the trick."

"There's always someone named Bill."

"And if there hadn't been?"

"Then I would have looked all embarrassed and said I probably had the name wrong. *'I'm terrible with names,'*" he mimicked.

We came to the first building. There was no sign, just some numbers up high on the corner of the wall near the roof. There was a small parking lot with only a few cars in it. The one-way road ran parallel to the path, disappearing into the trees beyond the first building.

The second building was surprisingly large for the setting, a square, warehouse structure with an impressive wire fence that ran past a small parking area and continued on around both sides of the building. The fence was at least eight feet high with barbed wire along the top. Through it I could make out the entrance in the distance. We found a gate to the parking lot, but it didn't move when we pushed at it. We hadn't expected it would. There was a keypad on a post next to the right side of the gate. You needed either the code or wire cutters to gain entry.

"Think there's a way in around to the side?" I asked.

"If this fence is any indication, I doubt it. Doesn't look like they want visitors."

Just then we saw a man come out of the entrance across the parking area and head in our direction. He had a phone in his hand and kept looking around as he walked toward us, as if checking to make sure we were alone. He stopped on the other side of the gate and said, "You Logan and Bryn?"

"Yes," I said. "And you're Bill."

"I don't remember Jared mentioning you. Or any camping trip."

"To be honest," I began, ignoring Logan's warning glare. "I met Jared while hiking in Scotland. We were staying at the same inn. And being Seattleites, we kinda hit it off. We'd made arrangements to get together again toward the end of his trip, but he didn't show. Now I can't get in touch with him here. It seems odd."

Bill looked me up and down. "You don't look like Jared's type." His tone was more factual than rude, but I didn't feel like it was a compliment.

"What can I say? We bonded over midges and mud on a hike."

Logan jumped in. "If you're hinting that Jared doesn't want to get together with Bryn, this seems like a pretty elaborate brush-off to me." He paused and furrowed his brow at Bill, a teaching ploy to let a student know he was being tested. "Is there some reason you won't tell us whether he's okay?"

Bill looked uncomfortable but didn't respond to Logan's question directly. "Look, we have tight security here, and I have no way of knowing if you're using this story as a ploy to try to get inside."

"Why would we do that?" Logan asked, sounding sincerely puzzled.

Bill looked from me to Logan and back to me again. Finally, he said, "Logan didn't return to work when I expected him to, so I called the hotel where he was staying. They told me he had extended his vacation."

"Doesn't it seem strange to you that he would do that without letting someone at work know?" I asked.

"No stranger than you two showing up here asking questions."

Logan and I exchanged looks. "Okay," I said. "There's more to it than we've said. I did, ah, run across Jared in Scotland. And I'm concerned that something may have happened to him." I looked to Logan for support, and he obligingly jumped in.

"It might be better to talk about this somewhere less conspicuous. Maybe we could meet you after work?"

"You're not with some protest group, are you?"

"No." I dug in my purse. "Here's my card." I poked it through the fence. He took it and studied it as if it could tell him whether I was a real person or a fake.

"And here's mine," Logan said, turning his card sideways to get it through the odd-shaped chain-link openings. Bill accepted Logan's card and put it through the same scrutiny as he had mine. He didn't walk away, but he didn't look convinced either. "You can check me out on the UW website," Logan added. "We can meet you wherever you want. What do you say?"

As he stood there staring at us, I could practically hear the argument he was having with himself. On the one hand, he was undoubtedly worried that we were a couple of anti-chimera crackpots. On the other hand, he had to be worried about his colleague.

Finally, he agreed to meet us for drinks at a local cafe and wine bar after work. Without saying anything more, he turned and headed back toward his workplace.

"They are certainly wary of visitors," Logan said as we headed back up the path.

"It makes me wonder just what *is* going on in that building."

if pigs could fly . . . and think

Logan and I returned to the marina, and I went to my office to catch up on what I had missed while I was gone. My office is in a small room on the second floor of a three-story wood building at the foot of the dock. There's a short flight of stairs from the road above the marina to the dock below with a platform leading to the offices at street level on the second floor. All of the offices have sloping wood floors and old fixtures that show their age. But the rent is relatively cheap, and my office has the extra plus of having a peek-a-boo view of the lake.

When I opened the door and went inside, I was almost disappointed to see that everything looked just like I'd left it—cluttered desk, bookshelves filled to capacity and then some, a well-used Keurig on a wobbly end table in the corner. The only thing missing was my goldfish, Bubbles II. My landlord, Hudson Hiller, had reluctantly agreed to pet sit while I was gone. The original goldfish had been an unwanted gift, and I had refused to give it a name because of my experience with short-lived pets when I was young. But my niece, Emma, insisted that pets needed names. Unfortunately, the day she christened the fish "Bubbles," it had died. The current "Bubbles" is my way of avoiding having to disappoint Emma. Only a few people know the fish is really Bubbles II.

I'd been checking email while in Scotland, so there were no real surprises waiting for me. But there was a long list of things I had agreed to do when I returned. Somehow two and a half weeks ago the list hadn't seemed overwhelming, but it sure did now. I groaned as I sat down in my chair, cleared a space around my laptop, and logged in.

The afternoon flew by in a flurry of emails, telephone calls, promises to do this or that, occasional visits from Macavity demanding attention and treats. And a visit from my landlord.

"You back?" he said, poking his head around the door after I'd yelled "Come on in."

"I thought it might be you," I said.

Hudson stepped inside. It came as no surprise that he was holding a fishbowl. But there was no fish in it.

"Oh, not again." I moaned.

"I'm so sorry. Maybe I overfed it"

"It isn't your fault," I assured him.

"I was going to get you another one, but I wasn't sure if you'd want it."

"I don't." Supposedly goldfish can live up to 45 years, but you can't prove it by me. "Maybe it's time Emma learns to deal with loss."

Hudson, a tall man in his early 60s with several grandchildren he adores, and a soft spot for children in general, quickly assured me that wouldn't be necessary. "I'll pick up one for you tomorrow."

We argued back and forth a bit about who would purchase the new "Bubbles" before I gave in. Bubbles III would take up residence in my office the next afternoon. Maybe I should accept the inevitable and quit counting.

Logan and I arrived at the café and wine bar right on the dot; Bill was already there, waiting for us at a table near the side window. He was good looking in a nondescript sort of way—

brown hair, brown checked shirt, dark-rimmed glasses. Not someone you would notice in a crowd, but not someone you would avoid at a party.

He waved us over and nodded as we seated ourselves across from him. The waitress appeared as if by magic and took our drink orders. Then the three of us stared at each other, waiting for someone to take the lead.

"I'm afraid I have bad news," I began. I'd decided he needed to hear the truth. So, I went through what had happened and explained that the police were convinced that Jared was still alive, but that I was just as sure that he wasn't. The only thing I left out was my feeling that there might have been someone in the ravine with me. It sounded so paranoid. "I'm so sorry to have to tell you this," I concluded.

Bill looked stricken. He sat there, absolutely still. I waited, feeling uncomfortable with the silence but unable to think of anything to add. Logan, too, remained silent. Finally, Bill said,

"What I can't understand is what he was doing on that trail."
"What do you mean?" Logan asked.

"Jared wasn't a nature lover, and he definitely wasn't a hiker."
I suddenly remembered his tennis shoes. Real hikers don't wear tennis shoes in the rain.

"Then why was he in Scotland?"
Bill took a deep breath. "Jared went to Scotland to meet with a researcher he's been in contact with. He wanted to see for himself what the guy was working on. The guy is in a small private lab near the place where Jared was staying."

"I take it that he and this other scientist were working on similar projects?"

"Yes."

When he didn't continue, I said, "I assume your work is for some reason being kept secret, but can I ask if you think it could be related to Jared's death?"

"You think it wasn't an accident?" Bill seemed more upset than surprised.

"Is there a reason someone would want to harm Jared? Someone who would know about his trip to Scotland?"

Bill sighed and took a long swig of whatever it was he was drinking. "He was just finishing an experiment on . . . well, let's just say it involved a gestation period. He thought he had enough time to get to Scotland and back before the results were in. And . . . well, there's a problem." He hesitated, clearly trying to decide how much to tell us. "I don't understand why you two are asking questions. Why not just tell the police here what you know?"

I leaned back, grappling with his question, not sure I knew the answer myself. "I feel somewhat . . . ah, responsible. Not for his death, but for how I handled what happened when I found him. And I don't think the police will do anything for a while. Jared did, after all, supposedly call the inn and say he was extending his trip. *You* might be able to light a fire under them, but I keep thinking that if we had a few more facts, that might encourage an investigation."

Logan jumped in. "You're obviously concerned about security issues at work. And I remember the protest and fire at NorPac. Feelings ran pretty high. Do you think these same protesters could be involved?"

Bill shook his head. "I just don't know."

"What's the 'problem' that you referred to?" I asked.

Bill blinked a few times and took another deep breath. "Look," he said, "I can't give you any details, but I can tell you that Jared was pretty secretive about his research. Even within our group. We've had information leaked before. We've been hacked, had attempted break-ins, you name it. I haven't been working on Jared's project, but he and I talked as much as anyone. So with him missing and his computer gone . . ."

"Did he have his computer with him in Scotland?" Logan asked.

"I don't know. He usually leaves it in the safe at the office and takes his tablet. That's our protocol. But it isn't there. I assume he took it with him."

"So, what's happening to the project he was working on?"

"I'm trying to record what I *think* he was looking for. But I don't have the comparative data. And, to be honest, Jared was a genius. It's going to take some doing to get up to speed on his work."

"Is it time sensitive?"

"Yes and no. It may already be too late to reap the benefits from his latest experiment. But it can be repeated. If I can figure out exactly what he was doing. Of course, as soon as the company finds out Jared won't be returning, they will probably throw every resource they have at it to try and recreate Jared's experiment. It's potentially a big-time medical breakthrough. On the other hand, you don't miss what you don't have, if you know what I mean."

"This scientist in Scotland, how much do you know about what he is up to?"

"Not much."

"Have you tried contacting him?"

"I haven't. But I will." He glanced at his iPhone. "They're what, eight hours ahead of our time? So, if I call them when I get up, I might get through to him."

"Sounds good." I paused, then thought, what the hell? "Here's what I think you should ask him." I launched into a string of questions I thought he should pursue. First, he should find out what the guy knew about Jared's movements while in the area. Had he met with Jared, and if so, when? Did Jared tell him anything about going anywhere else before heading home? Was he meeting with anyone else? Second, did he seem nervous or express any concerns about his safety? Third, did he have a laptop or tablet with him, or both? And, finally, I wanted him to ask if there was anything, anything at all, that they had talked about that might provide a clue as to Jared's whereabouts.

Bill actually smiled. "I can see that you have the mind of an investigator."

"Some people just think she's pushy," Logan said.

"It's my training," I said, perhaps a bit defensively. "Organizational development consultants are in the problem-solving business," I explained. "Most clients come to you because they need help figuring something out or strategizing about what to do next to reach their goals. It involves asking a lot of questions and searching for connections."

"And being persistent, like a dog on a scent," Logan added.

"Which brings me back to what Jared was working on," I said. "Is there anyone in the scientific community with reason to want to destroy or slow down this research? Or would it be more likely that he would be attacked by someone opposed to either his specific project or the use of animals in experiments?"

"Again, I'm not sure. There are a lot of ignorant people out there who fear that we are going to create some sort of hybrid monster. That we will start blurring the distinction between man and animal. But that's not what we're trying to do. We are looking for medical solutions to save human lives." He sounded passionate about their mission, then suddenly looked deflated. "So many people just don't understand," he said. "They think we're wild-eyed crazies who are completely out of touch with 'normal' people. The movies are full of mad scientists, and a lot of people buy into the stereotype."

As he talked, I thought about how normal he looked. Definitely not the mad scientist of film fame. But then, if we were right about what HHC was up to, Jared and his colleagues were pushing the limits of known science by experimenting with human DNA and animals. Sane or insane? It depended on your point of view. But in any case, it seemed to me like it could be a pretty good motive for murder.

home sweet home

Logan and Judd had plans for the evening, so I found myself home alone with a can of jalapeno chili and a cat. The crackers were stale. And I didn't have any cheese or onions. I really needed to go shopping. Macavity agreed: I was out of his favorite snack food, and he wasn't going to give me any peace until I remedied the situation.

Then Sophie called and wanted to know why I hadn't got in touch. Was I still upset because she hadn't gone with me? No, I explained, things had just been a little hectic since I returned. She gushed a little about how much she was looking forward to telling me all about her "latest guy," Jason or Jackson or Jeremy, something like that. I said I couldn't wait. I was lying, of course, but we made plans to get together the following evening for dinner. There was going to be a lot to catch up on.

Next it was my mother's turn to berate me for not checking in. "Mom," I whined, "I haven't even been back 24 hours yet." She always brings out the pre-teen whiner in me. "I have jet lag." I yawned loudly to prove my point. Then she made me promise to come to Sunday dinner with the family. As if anyone could forget that we all have dinner together the first Sunday of the month. "I have jet lag, not dementia," I said. "Of course, I'll be there."

"You could have sent a postcard," she said pointedly just before she hung up. I had sent messages via email and posted pictures on Facebook, but apparently that wasn't good enough. Well, the trinkets I'd brought back for everyone might make up for it. That had been one advantage of being a tourist instead of a hiker. I had done a lot of shopping.

Ignoring my still protesting cat, I set my alarm for 8:00 am and went to bed.

My cell started blasting out a version of frogs partying in a pond at 6:30 am. I really needed to change my ringtone. Macavity jumped on my chest to let me know I needed to answer immediately. Either he was looking out for my best interests or he was annoyed by the frogs having fun. I pushed him aside, grabbed my phone, swiped my finger across the base and mumbled a hello. The phone kept ringing. I opened one eye and saw that I had the phone upside down. I turned it around and swiped again.

Bill said, "I hope I didn't wake you up." No one who says that ever means it, and the person on the receiving end usually feels obliged to deny they were sleeping. I was no exception.

"I was just getting up." My alarm wouldn't go off for another hour and a half, but he didn't need to know that.

"You said as soon as I talked to Rory McKnight, I should let you know."

"Is that the scientist Jared went to meet?"

"Yes. I just got off the phone with him."

"And . . .?" I sat up and swung my legs over the side of the bunk, trying to get my mind to focus.

"He said Jared didn't show for their meeting."

"Did he try to get in touch with him?"

"When he called the inn, he was told the same thing they told me, that Jared had extended his hiking trip. He thought it was odd, but he figured Jared would be in touch eventually. But he hasn't been." He paused. "One other thing . . . Rory thought maybe Jared had decided he didn't want to talk to him after all. Apparently, Rory has some concerns about how Jared is, er, was handling his research."

"Really?" That put another twist on things.

"He didn't want to go into detail with me this morning but suggested we have a conference call to discuss protocols before anyone proceeds with Jared's work."

"Sounds serious."

"I'm going to check him out and make sure he's someone we should be listening to. It could be a question of wanting to beat us to the punch. Science versus money to be made, you know."

"Well, if you would keep me in the loop, I'd appreciate it." Bill promised to do so, and we ended the call.

I got back into my bunk, thoroughly intending to take a few minutes to think about this latest development. But the next thing I knew my alarm was telling me it was 8:00 and it really was time to get up. I told myself it was already 4:00 pm in Scotland, but my body didn't know what to think.

I dragged myself up, made a cup of coffee, and called Fiona. I had texted her the night before to expect my call, so she answered on the second ring.

"Bryn," she said, sounding far too chipper for my morning before-coffee state of mind.

"Fiona," I mumbled.

"You don't sound very awake."

"Just got up. Thought I wouldn't be able to sleep."

"You're lucky. It takes me a week to get my body back on local time when I travel."

"Yeah, lucky." I took a sip of coffee.

"So, did you check on whether Jared Blaine showed up at work?"

"He didn't."

"Bloody hell, as my English friends would say."

"Yeah, not a good sign. And he was supposed to meet with a

local scientist in Scotland, but a colleague of Blaine's checked, and he didn't show up for his appointment.

"Apparently, that was the reason for the trip in the first place. Not to go hiking in tennis shoes in the rain. Did I mention he was wearing tennis shoes?"

"Bloody hell," she repeated, this time more soulfully.

"And . . .," I paused to take another sip of coffee. "I'm beginning to suspect that there were any number of people who might have wanted him dead. It seems he was engaged in rather controversial scientific research."

"Do you think someone followed him to Scotland? Or is it possible we have a home-grown bad guy?"

"It could even be a matter of someone in the States working with someone in your country. There are a lot of people opposed to what he was doing." I gave her a brief overview of the general nature of his research, including what Bill had mentioned about the potential financial bonanza for being the first to make a breakthrough. "That could explain why someone wanted to delay his body being discovered," I concluded. "Maybe there's another scientist on the verge of making a similar announcement. If he—or she—can keep Blaine's death under wraps for a while, that could delay HHG's efforts to come up to speed on what Blaine was doing. I understand he was pretty secretive about his experiment, even within his own company."

"Hmmm. That makes sense. But wouldn't it become obvious once the other scientist's research is published and Blaine's body discovered?"

"Yes. Maybe too obvious. But there has to be a reason why someone didn't want the body discovered right away. That's assuming, of course, that it eventually turns up."

"So . . . what would you like me to do at this end?"

"Can you check out your local scientist, Rory McKnight? See what his reputation is and get a feel for what he's like as a person? Also, you might try to find out if there is anyone or any group there that is upset about this kind of research."

"I'll get on it right away."

"Great. I'll get back to you in a day or so, okay?"

"And if I learn anything earthshaking, I'll give you a shout."

"Is that a Scottish saying—'I'll give you a shout'?"

She laughed. "I was trying to impress you with my colloquial English. I did get it right, didn't I?"

"Yes, you did." I laughed and said, "I learned a few Scottish idioms on the airplane on the way over, but I wasn't too successful using them. 'Hou's yer dous'?" I said.

"What?"

"Does my pronunciation suck?"

"Not if you intended to ask me about my pigeons."

"Damn, I thought I was saying 'how's it going?'"

Fiona laughed. "So how many people did you ask about their pigeons while you were here?"

I groaned, remembering the smiles and the head shaking.

"Don't worry, they probably appreciated that you tried."

still besties

The day went by in a flash. I love my work, but sometimes I think it would be nice to be independently wealthy. Well, that's not entirely true, I *often* think it would be nice to never have to worry about money. But I don't need to make a lot. I live frugally and don't collect many material possessions. You can't when you live on a boat. Not if you want to be able to cast off on a moment's notice and go sailing. Still, I've accumulated a locker full of things I never look at and will probably never use. Go figure.

Just before I went home to change for dinner my landlord came by with Bubbles III. "I hope he looks the same," he said. Hudson is a good landlord and a kind person.

"They are hard to tell apart," I assured him.

"I don't know." He shook his head. "Kids can be pretty observant."

I peered at the goldfish. "No distinguishing marks," I said. "Same size. Same color. I think he can pass." Hudson looked relieved, and I thanked him profusely for extending the family line.

After he left, I cleared a space for the bowl on one of my cluttered shelves. "Don't die on me," I pleaded with Bubbles III, "and

I'll get you some fresh seaweed, maybe a cute little plastic treasure chest. How would you like that?" With enough junk in the bowl Emma might not look too closely at its latest resident. Although if she detected some changes, I could always say that Bubbles was aging. That would be the truth; we're all aging.

That evening Sophie and I met at our favorite restaurant. It's a small, casual place with comfortable seating in the bar. We usually eat in the bar because there's no pressure there to hurry through your meal, and they never seem to care if you linger over a glass or two of wine.

We did our usual A-frame hug. I'm quite a bit taller than her, so I have to bend over to give her a hug. Sophie is short and shapely with lovely chestnut colored hair. She was the popular one in high school, the yell leader with lots of boyfriends. I, on the other hand, had a reputation for being smart, labeled "the most likely to succeed" in our annual. Not something most young girls aspire to in high school. Even so, proximity and shared teen-age traumas had resulted in Sophie and me becoming fast friends.

Even after we left home, Sophie and I had sustained our friendship. Through our college years at different schools, through my wanderings and her marriage. And through all of the rest of our ups and downs. Her miscarriage and eventual divorce. My failed relationships and mother problems. Everything life threw at us we were there for each other. So, even though I was still a bit peeved that she had chosen a man over our vacation plans, there was no way a few midges and a dead body were going to break that bond.

As soon as we ordered, Sophie turned to me and asked, "So what happened over there?"

"What makes you think something 'happened'?" Sophie has always been good at reading me. She smiled and shook her head. "Fess up." From experience, I knew it would be no use to try to hold out, even for a short period of time. I was no match for Sophie's determination; I spilled the whole story from finding the body to what Logan and I had learned about Blaine and his research, talking non-stop until I reached the end.

When I finished, she asked, "So what are we going to do now?"

"'We'?" I asked.

"You and Logan are obviously going to keep trying to figure out what happened to Blaine, and I would like to help. It's the least I can do."

"Because you weren't there with me, you mean?"

"Yes, and because I have a connection that might be useful."

"What kind of 'connection'?"

"Ever heard of the 'Say No to Chimeras' group?"

"That's an actual group?"

"I know, strange name, but 'yes.' Someone I know at work is a member. He started protesting the use of animals in research and then got involved in trying to stop using animals to grow human organs. He's really passionate about it."

"Is this an organized group? I mean, do they get together, have regular meetings?"

"I can find out."

Sophie had to go to work the next morning, and my jet lag started to kick in, so we made an early night of it. When I pulled into my parking space that looks out over the marina, I turned off the engine and sat there a few minutes taking in the view. The marina is sandwiched between two other maritime businesses, a boat builder on one side and a huge shipping warehouse on the other. Most of the buildings have been there for a long time and have the dilapidated look of structures destined for demolition. I hoped I wouldn't be there for the inevitable day when they were replaced by expensive waterfront condominiums.

Unlike some of the upscale marinas in the area, there are no locked gates where I moor my boat. As I walked down the dimly lit dock, I felt both comfortable and uneasy at the same time.

Living alone at the end of a long pier has its advantages, but it can sometimes be unsettling. Tonight, even the shadows had shadows. The aging wood planks creaked. Sailboat rigging clanked in the evening breeze. Corrugated roofing rattled. Distant voices and activity drifted over the water and slowly blended in with the other night sounds. Familiar sounds, nothing out of place. No hulking figures lurking in the gloomy nooks and crannies on the finger floats. Nevertheless, I was relieved to reach the *Aspara* and find only Macavity waiting for me.

Up in my office the next morning I chatted on the phone with a couple of clients, set up a few meetings, and settled back into my normal life. Then I got a call from Sophie. The Say No to Chimeras group was meeting that very evening. Sophie was bummed that she had a prior commitment but told me that her contact would vouch for me. "His name is Conrad Tosh," she said. "He'll meet you at the door."

"Sounds like a Russian spy," I said.

"Oh, and remember, no one uses last names at these meetings."

"Really?"

"Conrad told me that sometimes they discuss activities that could be considered illegal."

Why didn't that surprise me?

Logan dropped by late afternoon and was both pleased and worried that I was going to a Say No to Chimeras meeting. No surprise that he wanted to come with me. But we both knew it was a bad idea. On my own I might be able to blend in. If there were two of us, we could draw unwanted attention. I gave him the address for the meeting, and we looked it up on Google Maps. It was in the basement of an aging church. The upstairs had recently been turned into a homeless shelter, but the basement was still available for public meetings.

"In that neighborhood you'll be lucky if your tires aren't stolen," Logan commented.

"That's not a politically correct comment," I pointed out.

"I'm just saying it's a high crime area, so you need to be careful."

"I'll take my pepper spray," I assured him. Although I'd actually taken a class on how to use the stuff, I thought the chances of spraying myself instead of an attacker were about 50-50. If I could get it out of my purse in time, that is.

I arrived a few minutes early and found a spot to park near the church. The building needed paint. You could see bare wood under peeling ribbons of dirty white. And what used to be a cultivated garden along the sidewalk was a jumble of unkempt bushes and weeds. In the front yard I could make out several tents and shopping carts filled with what someone considered worthy of hauling around. I felt a pang of guilt for not doing more to help those in need of a handout and a place to sleep.

There were several others arriving for the meeting. At least that's what I assumed based on their dress and the fact that they were walking purposefully toward the church. As I got out of my car, a young man in baggy jeans and a T-shirt with a picture of a sheep knitting from its own wool stepped in front of me. "Can I help you?" he asked officiously. He was unshaven, but his hair was stylishly straggly.

"I'm here for the meeting. Conrad is supposed to meet me at the door."

"You know Conrad?" He looked me up and down. I couldn't help but wonder if he was checking me out for himself or assessing whether I looked like someone Conrad might be dating. Either way, it made me uncomfortable.

"He's a friend of a friend," I said.

He fell into step beside me. Turning to a woman coming up behind us he said, "Shawna, see if you can find Conrad for me, okay?" She nodded and hurried off.

"So," he said, "how did you get interested in chimera research?"

"Ah, through reading about the misuse of animals in labs." I had prepared for the question, but I had been hoping no one would probe too deeply, and this guy seemed like he was going to do just that.

"Are you more concerned with animal protection than with organ incubation?"

"I'm opposed to both," I said. Fortunately, I was saved from further interrogation by the approach of a very short man in cutoffs and a green polo shirt. He was cute rather than handsome, and he walked with the confidence of someone who is sure of himself and of his place in the world. But I doubted that it would be with a woman almost six feet tall. Although it wasn't impossible. Still, I could feel my shoulders hunch as I tried to diminish my height, a habit I'd formed years ago and have never managed to completely shake.

"You Bryn?" he asked as he drew near.

"Conrad?"

He nodded and motioned for me to follow him. I gave the suspicious young man a smile and went with Conrad.

About twenty people were milling about when we went inside. It was a big room with fold-up chairs placed in a large circle. There would be no place to hide in this group even if they only used first names. Conrad acknowledged a few people as he led me to a seat, but he didn't introduce me to anyone. It was a youngish crowd overall with a few gray-haired men and women who looked like former hippies. I felt overdressed in my jeans and LL Bean shirt, and I was having trouble deciding how interested I should appear to be in the other attendees. People glanced in my direction, but no one seemed particularly inclined to find out who I was. I wondered what would have happened if I had wandered in without an escort.

Conrad left me and went over to talk to a small group of people on the other side of the room. A couple of them surreptitiously looked in my direction, so I suspected he was telling them about me. I half expected to have a bouncer come over and ask me to leave. But a few minutes later Conrad returned, and the meeting got under way.

I was surprised when it started with a reading of minutes from the previous meeting. I hadn't expected anything that organized, and I definitely hadn't anticipated that they were keeping a written record of their activities.

Several people gave updates on research currently in progress and named the scientists and companies involved. It was pretty much what I had read online. Then someone made a comment that surprised me.

"There's a rumor going around that a local scientist has gone missing." The speaker was a young woman with a mass of brown curls framing an oval face and big brown eyes. "Jared Blaine," she said. "*The* Jared Blaine."

"He's that bastard from the NorPac lab, right?" someone asked. A mumbling of agreement made its way around the circle. Whether they were agreeing he was from NorPac or a bastard—or both—wasn't clear.

I wanted to ask how she had found out that he was missing, but that didn't seem to fit with the low profile I was trying to maintain.

Conrad spoke up. "I've got him on the list. I'll follow up. Check with me after the meeting, Maureen, okay?"

I wondered what "list" Jared was on. I was fairly certain it wasn't a reminder to send him a birthday card.

The last item on the agenda was about the protest they were organizing for Saturday afternoon in front of City Hall.

"Why Saturday?" I whispered to Conrad. There weren't any officials around on Saturday.

"It's when we can get the most volunteers together," Conrad whispered back.

When they asked for volunteers to make signs, I held up my hand, and they took down my first name. When they asked for volunteers to protest, I held up my hand again, not sure if I really wanted to participate or not. But it seemed like a good way to show I was supportive of the cause. It did, however, cross my mind that I might not want to be seen on television carrying one of the signs I had just volunteered to make.

The sign making was going to take place in the room we were in on the following evening. They had the supplies lined up; they just needed volunteers to do the work.

When the meeting ended, I thanked Conrad and exited along with several others. No one made eye contact or talked to me. I certainly hoped they would be more chatty over sign making the next evening.

coincidence? i think not!

Thursday morning, I was in my bunk, resisting the thought of getting up. The sun was streaming through the tiny porthole, creating a circle of light on the opposite bunk. Macavity was curled in the center of the circle, the dark swirls on his side in stark contrast to the orange fur that covered most of his body. He considered the bunk his and pushed clothes aside when I carelessly tossed them there.

As I watched him, he suddenly stretched, his paws extending beyond the circle of sunlight. Then he opened his green eye and glared at me. It wasn't time to get up yet.

Unfortunately, I had work to do, so I braved his irritation and hauled myself up. He gave me one last hostile glance for disturbing him and curled up again, his tail flicking a few times as if he was saying, "get on with it if you must, but I'm staying right where I am."

Fiona called just as I was about to leave for my office. She got right to the point. "Our scientist has a stellar reputation. Unlike yours."

"So, it's 'ours' and 'yours' now, is it?"

"Sorry. I'll use names, okay? Rory McKnight appears to be a respected scientist, published in tons of journals, with quite a few articles on ethical norms for research. I browsed the titles and skimmed a few summaries. He's particularly interested in things that may be legal but are still considered by many as unethical. He's also written about intellectual property issues, cooperation among scientists, and peer review, to name a few. His main themes seem to be social responsibility and what he terms 'ethical reflection.' And he had a recent article that talked about how researchers who use animal subjects need to be held accountable not only for the humane treatment of animals but for carefully weighing value against potential risks. He addressed specific concerns about stem cell research."

"He mention any names?"

"No, but Jared Blaine's name surfaced in a twitter exchange between a local group of scientists."

"Scientists tweet?"

"They do in the UK." Fiona laughed. "One referred to Blaine as a 'turd.' The ultimate label of distain in Scotland."

"So, McKnight might have been intending to have a 'come to Jesus' meeting with Blaine. Scientist to scientist. Hmmm. Maybe push came to shove," I speculated.

"I hope not," Fiona said. "I think McKnight is the kind of watchdog scientist we need."

After a quick stop at my office to feed Bubbles III, I hopped in my car to head to a 10:30 a.m. meeting with a client. Miraculously, traffic was light, and I arrived early. I estimated I could grab a cup of coffee and still be on time. Since there are coffee shops on almost every corner in Seattle, it isn't surprising that half the population of the city walk around with paper coffee cups or commuter mugs, like extensions of their hands. Strangely enough, I seldom see anyone actually take a drink.

There were only three people ahead of me in line, but the woman before me had one of those orders that require a half shot of this, a pump of that, skinny something, soy something else, and so on. It makes me want to scream something stupid, like "what's wrong with just ordering coffee?!" Not that there was any room in her cup for any actual coffee. By the time I placed my order for a grande drip, I was starting to worry about my timing.

As I turned away from the counter, I almost collided with a man studying the reader board. He stepped back just in time. We both apologized at once. Then I realized who it was. The man I'd met in the parking lot in Scotland.

"Keith!"

"Bryn." He smiled, his bright blue eyes alight with pleasure, the cleft on his chin accentuated by the upturn of his mouth. "What are you doing here?" I asked at the same time he said, "What a pleasant surprise." With his brogue, the comment came across as a verbal hug.

"What . . .," I started again as he laughed.

"Have time to drink that here?" he asked, nodding at my cup.

"No, I'm late for a meeting."

"What about after?"

"Sure," I said. "I should be through by 11:30 or so."

"Why don't we meet back here then? If you're a little late, I'll wait." He gave me another dimpled smile.

As I hurried off to my meeting, I couldn't help but wonder about the answer to my question—what was he doing here?

Coincidence? In a book by Nabokov there's a story about a man who loses a diamond cufflink in the sea and exactly twenty years later to the day he is eating a fish . . . and there is no diamond inside. On the other hand, there could have been.

I managed to put Keith out of my mind during most of the meeting. But an extreme sense of unease played at the back of my consciousness. If he'd been planning a trip to the US, why hadn't he mentioned it when we met in Scotland? And if it had been a last-minute thing, could he have orchestrated our meeting? Did he want to see me again, or was he in some way connected to Blaine's disappearance? Was it possible there lurked a cold-blooded killer behind those Robert Redford eyes and Ben Affleck chin?

When the meeting was over, I was tempted to skip returning

to Starbucks. Curiosity battled with suspicion. Finally, I called Logan. But instead of sage advice, I got his message: "Leave your name and number and I'll probably call you back." I've told him how annoying his message is, but he claims it's honest. I almost hung up; instead, I made the decision to meet Keith and told Logan when and where so someone would know where to start looking for me if I disappeared. It was a melodramatic thought, but it didn't seem totally paranoid under the circumstances.

Keith was there when I arrived, standing up to give me a hug like we were old friends. Then he asked what I wanted to drink, and I sat down and watched while he went to the counter, made the order, and, if I wasn't mistaken, flirted with the barista. Since his back was to me, I couldn't tell for sure, but she was certainly turning on the charm, and he didn't seem to be doing anything to discourage her.

While I waited, I took out my phone and texted Fiona. "You won't believe who I'm having coffee with—Keith." When she didn't immediately text me back, I was disappointed. Oh well, I could text or even call her later when I had a better feel for why Keith was in town.

"So," he said as he set my coffee down in front of me, "you miss Scotland?"

"Just the midges."

"What about your midge protector?" He was definitely in flirt mode.

I took a sip of coffee. "What about you? On a business trip? Or pleasure?"

"It started as business." He smiled. "Now . . .?"

"Seriously, you didn't mention a trip to the US."

"No, it was a last-minute thing."

"And I don't think you've mentioned what you do for a living." During our conversation in Scotland I'd done most of the talking. He'd done the listening. What little I knew about him I'd learned from Fiona.

"I'm in marketing," he said.

"So, you're marketing something in the US?"

"Scotch, what else?" He got out a card and handed it to me.

"Family business?" Fiona had mentioned something about his family's "connections."

"Well, yes, as a matter of fact." Did his eyes narrow slightly, or was it my imagination?

"And are you trying to do mass marketing or just boutique sales?" I wasn't sure whether my question made sense, but I wanted to hear him talk about his alleged business trip. For some reason I couldn't put my finger on I was becoming more and more convinced he was in the area because of Jared Blaine. Maybe it was that he was just too perfect to be real.

"There are a couple of local retailers interested. I'm here to gauge whether it makes sense for us or not. But enough about business, what have you been up to since you got home?"

"Just settling back into my routine. Replacing my goldfish. He died while I was gone," I explained. "And I don't want to disappoint my niece." He nodded as if it all made perfect sense to him. "Dinner with friends. That sort of thing."

"And did you learn any more about your missing hiker?" he asked. Well, that didn't take him long. He either underestimated my suspicious nature or overestimated his own charm. Maybe a little of both.

I paused, then said, "No, and I don't suppose I'll hear anything now that I'm home. Was there anything in the news about him in Scotland?"

"No, I just remembered how upset you were. I hoped you were able to put the experience behind you."

"Absolutely. I'm sure it was like everyone said—he came to and took off. I'm embarrassed that I made such a big deal out of it."

He reached over and put his hand on mine. "Emotions are a good thing." I felt a surge of warmth. He was good, really good.

"Thank you," I said as if he had given me permission to "feel."

We began chatting about the weather, the price of coffee and other neutral subjects. It was a comfortable conversation, but not one to encourage moving to another level of friendship. I hesitated to ask how long he was staying or where he was staying for fear he would think I wanted to see him again.

Finally, I glanced at my watch. "Well, I'm afraid I have to get going. I have some work to do before I meet a friend for dinner." Too much detail, I told myself as I stood up. "It was great running into you."

"Yes, it was good seeing you." He smiled that 100-watt smile again and took my empty cup from me. "I'll get rid of that for you."

Not a very romantic closing line, but it was all I got. I smiled back at 40 watts and left, briefly wondering if he was going to come on to the barista again. But I didn't care, did I?

CHAPTER 11

i protest!

Thursday evening, I went back to the church to help make signs for Saturday's demonstration. This time I had to park further away and found myself feeling self-conscious and a little frightened as I passed by a group of young men whose unkempt appearance screamed "homeless" to me. I remembered my grandfather reminiscing about how romantic it had been in his day to "ride the rails." And how he had known men "down on their luck," a temporary state. The chronically homeless were either less visible then or easier to ignore. Perhaps pitied but not feared. I chided myself for being nervous and acknowledged the young men with a nod as I went by. I got a few catcalls for my effort.

At the foot of the steps to the church I ran into some of the other volunteers. They seemed more relaxed than they had the night before, as though they were looking forward to an evening of shared work. As I fell into step alongside them, I was greeted with subdued but cordial head nods. But no one addressed me directly. I nodded back and kept my mouth shut. This was a tough group to break into.

The chairs had been cleared out of the room. In one corner there were stacks of cardboard and colored sheets of poster board, a collection of yard sticks, piles of markers, a heap of rulers, several cans of spray paint, rolls of colored masking tape, and a box of assorted odds and ends. Everyone seemed to know what was expected of them, except me. They quickly picked up what they wanted and headed for a space to start on their signs. I caught the eye of one of the women and asked, "What are we supposed to write on them?"

She looked at me as if seeing me for the first time. "You new to the group?" she asked.

"Yes."

"Ever been to a protest before?"

"Not one for this group."

Several other volunteers were now looking in my direction. I half expected someone to yell at me to leave. Instead, the woman I had asked shrugged and said, "Whatever you feel."

Whatever I "feel"? Great. I picked up some supplies and made my way to a vacant corner, trying to eye what others were doing on the way. Since they were just getting started, there wasn't much to go on.

Shortly after I knelt down a shadow fell across my blank poster board. A young man squatted on his haunches in front of me. He had on a plaid work shirt and jeans. His hair was well-trimmed, and, in spite of the casual clothes, he looked like someone who had a downtown office job during the day.

"Jan was right. We don't tell anyone what they should put on their signs. You can be very simplistic and direct or come up with something clever. Clever is good because it tends to get on the news. But as long as you spell everything correctly and don't write anything obscene, you can do whatever you want." He smiled. It was a nice smile. Friendly, but not too friendly. "The only other thing I would add is that you need to have enough white space to make the message easy to read." He stood up. "You'll get the hang of it."

"Thanks." I picked up a marker as if I now knew what I was

doing. Only I didn't. *Stop cell research on animals* wasn't going to cut it.

Then I had an idea. I had recently taught my niece, Emma, how to draw a pig using a few simple lines. It was something I had learned from a marketing guy who had given a workshop on how to create interesting flipcharts for presentations. I quickly drew a pig on its hind legs, put a thought bubble off to the side and wrote E=MC^2 in the bubble. Then I drew a large red circle around the picture with a diagonal line running from the top left to the bottom right.

As one of the other women passed by, she glanced down at my poster. She stopped suddenly and said, "Hey, I like that." She waved another woman over. A couple of others followed in her wake. "What do you think?" the first woman asked the second.

She didn't have to think long. "We could do a series of similar signs," she said. "What else can you draw?" she asked me.

"I'm afraid I have a limited repertoire," I admitted. "I'm not an artist." I looked around at the gathering group. "Maybe someone else here can draw animals."

"I can do some basic stuff," someone volunteered.

"I can work on what they are thinking," someone else offered. "Create some other math equations—so we have variety."

"Or we could have two animals talking to each other. A pig talking to a dog . . . or cat . . . or whatever."

"Two animals playing chess."

The ideas spewed forth. I was surprised how much they liked the idea; it wasn't exactly original. But having a sign theme for the protest was probably a good idea. *Way to go,* I said to myself. Too bad I wasn't trying to be helpful.

Everyone got into the swing of things and started sharing ideas and coordinating with each other. Some of the animal depictions weren't all that great, but you could tell what they were supposed to be. And a few of the thought bubbles were very clever. The fellow who said he could draw did a wonderful sign of two pigs playing chess. He did another of a cow that looked like it had stepped out of a Gary Larson cartoon strip. The cow was wearing a bow tie and top hat, miraculously holding a cane in its hoof, and doing a dance step. The caption read: "Cowbert captures Broadway."

It was almost eleven when we finished. We stacked the posters in piles near the door and sat down on the floor in a circle. Bags of cookies and chips were passed around. This seemed like the opportunity I'd been waiting for, but I didn't quite know how to broach the subject. Fortunately, someone did it for me.

"They learn anything yet about that missing scientist?" someone asked.

No one seemed to have any new information.

"Didn't someone say he works for NorPac?" I asked.

"A branch of it."

"Have you picketed them?" I asked. It seemed like a simple question, but everyone fell silent. You would have thought I'd asked whether they had burgled the place. Or tried to burn it down. "Sorry," I said. "Have I asked something I shouldn't?" Sometimes it pays to be straightforward. I was hoping this was one of those times.

"You know they've had, ah, problems," someone offered.

"I was just wondering about past protests." I tried to sound noncommittal.

"Yes, we've picketed them on numerous occasions. They are one of the worst offenders anywhere," the woman referred to as Jan offered with feeling.

"And the missing scientist is the worst of the worst," someone chimed in. "Totally out of control." There were murmurs of agreement.

Things would have been fine if someone hadn't brought up the fact that he'd gone missing in Scotland. And if they hadn't tricked me into saying that I'd been in Scotland recently. Okay, so they didn't actually trick me. Someone asked about the locale where he'd gone missing, and I'd volunteered where it was in Scotland. It was a short journey from sharing that bit of knowledge to admitting I'd been there. Recently. I thought about lying about the timing, but I wasn't sure if Sophie had mentioned the trip to Conrad or not. So I decided it was better to tell the truth. Probably not my best move of the evening.

The mood shifted dramatically. Suddenly the cookies and chips disappeared and people started getting to their feet. No one said anything to me, but it felt like I'd just admitted I had a pocket full of Zika bearing mosquitoes. Silently and in unison, they had collectively labeled me persona non grata.

As I made my way back to my car, one of the men from the group fell into step alongside me. The scowl on his face suggested that whatever he had to say, it wasn't going to be friendly. Without any preliminaries, he asked, "Do you work for NorPac?"

"No, I don't. Why would you think that?"

"Seems strange that you start coming to our meetings the week after one of their scientists goes missing in Scotland, and that by coincidence you were *visiting* there in the same place at the same time." He hit the word "visiting" hard, like it had some hidden meaning.

"Look," I said. "I don't have any connections with anyone in the medical research field. I don't approve of what some of these scientists are doing, and I just want to help."

He looked at me, his eyes narrowing. "Maybe you should forget about the protest on Saturday," he said. "You can check with Conrad about any future activities. Do I make myself clear?"

I could imagine why they might not want me at any future meetings, but why on earth would they bar me from the protest? I wanted to argue with him and to ask if he spoke for the entire group, but there was something about his tone that made me back off instead. "Okay. But I don't work for NorPac. Really."

I stopped just short of saying "believe me." I'd already lost the argument; I might as well just go home. I hadn't been looking forward to being part of their protest anyway.

He nodded and walked away, leaving me alone on a dark and deserted street. It occurred to me that if they asked the right people, they might be able to find out that I had reported finding Jared Blaine's body. And then they would wonder why I hadn't mentioned it the night before. Withholding that piece of information definitely suggested I had more of an agenda for attending their meetings than simply agreeing with their cause.

And somehow, I didn't think they would give me the benefit of the doubt as to the nature of that agenda.

The shadows at the marina seemed particularly sinister as I made my way down the dock. When Macavity jumped off a boat and landed in front of me, I screeched, then swore. "Don't do that, Macavity." He wound himself around my legs without any regard for the fright he'd given me. "Did you hear what I said?" I asked, my voice loud in the stillness of the night. There was no breeze, no creaking and groaning as vessels tugged at their moorings. Everything was totally silent. Like a graveyard at midnight.

Macavity pushed ahead of me when I pulled back the hatch and immediately attacked the dry cat food in his dish. He either sensed my mood or was too hungry to demand something better. I shut the hatch and locked it. Then, in spite of the hour, I called Sophie. She answered on the third ring.

"How'd it go?" she asked. I gave a brief overview of the first part of the evening and then admitted my blunder. "I'm sorry," I said. "I hope I haven't put Conrad in an awkward spot."

"Conrad can handle himself. But what about that guy who threatened you?"

"He didn't actually 'threaten' me."

"*Don't call us, we'll call you* doesn't exactly sound hospitable. Especially with a group used to skirting the law."

"What do you think they'll do if they find out I was the one to report him missing?"

Sophie thought for a moment. "It seems to me that your experience in Scotland can be the reason you inquired about the group. It doesn't automatically mean you are trying to find dirt on them. You could still be interested in their cause."

"That makes sense to me. Even if they decide that my only

reason for getting involved was to try to find out what happened to Blaine--. That surely isn't sinister in and of itself. Unless . . ."

"Yes, unless they are somehow involved in his disappearance." Sophie and I have always been able to finish each other's sentences. But this was one time I wished she'd disagreed with what I'd had in mind.

break-in!

When my phone frogs started partying, I opened one eye and looked at my clock: 6:30 a.m. Damn. I wasn't sure I could face what was probably not good news without a cup of coffee. And Macavity was clearly irked. His eyes were closed but he was swatting my phone with one paw, his tail flicking ominously. Before he could smack it off the bunk onto the floor, I grabbed it up and ended the party.

"Hello," I said. I hadn't even bothered to look at who was calling.

"Bryn, did I get you up?"

"That's okay, Bill. I'm sure you have a reason to be calling this early." Did my tone suggest that *he'd better have a damn good reason?*

"I thought you'd want to know," he began.

I sat partially up, my head brushing the low ceiling. "What's happened?"

"Someone broke in."

"At Humanity Health Group?"

"Yes."

His news jolted me into wakefulness. I rolled over on my side and propped myself up on one elbow. "But how?" It was a fortress; I couldn't imagine anyone breaking in there.

"I got here early this morning, 5:30," Bill said. "Couldn't sleep. The first thing I noticed was that the power was off. Even the back-up system. It still is. The power company sent someone over right away when I called. One of the men said the power went off around 2:00 a.m. Someone set off a small explosive charge that disconnected a nearby transformer. The whole neighborhood is out. It may take some time to get us back online. They also took out the security camera footage. It was a professional job."

"What was taken?"

"Nothing."

"Nothing?"

"Not that I know of. They broke in to destroy what was left of Jared's project. They burned the few notes he'd left behind, smashed all the equipment, destroyed the personal pictures he had on his desk, and killed the test animals. They even shredded his lab coats."

"They killed the test animals?" That didn't sound like something the "Say No" people would do. Although they couldn't necessarily know how close the animals were to assimilating human cells. So maybe it did make sense.

"A single shot through the head for the larger animals. A couple of the smaller rodents, well, let's just say there isn't much left."

"And they shredded his lab coats. Sounds like a pretty strong statement to me."

"The police are going over everything now. Thought I should warn you since they asked if anyone had shown any interest in Jared's work recently."

"You gave them my name . . . and Logan's," I said.

"I had to. But I made it clear that your only interest was in finding Jared."

"Did you tell them that I think Jared is dead?"

"Yes. I'm afraid I just blurted out the truth. I was so upset. I wasn't thinking clearly."

"That's all right, Bill. We have nothing to hide." At least I hoped I didn't.

We chatted a few more minutes. Bill didn't really know any more than he'd already told me, but he obviously needed to talk. I managed to calm him down a bit and suggested that Logan and I could meet him later to talk some more. He agreed to let me know when he was free, and we left it at that.

By the time I got up, put on the coffee, and got dressed, it was 7:00. Even at that hour I hesitated to call Logan. Although it was a workday for him, he often holds office hours instead of conducting classes on Fridays, starting around 9:30. He always said it was to accommodate students that he started late, but I suspected it was also an excuse to sleep in.

With my cup of coffee in front of me, I granted Logan a few more minutes of sleep time by calling Fiona first. When I got her voicemail, I kept my message simple: "There was a break-in at HHG; will know more later." Then I called her back and left another message: "Did you get my text about running into Keith? Think it was a coincidence?"

Asking Fiona about Keith made me wonder whether there was any connection between him and the break-in at HHG. Did he have the technical know-how to break into a building with tons of security in place? He wouldn't have had to do it by himself. He could have brought someone with him or hired it done by someone here. If Fiona was right, he had family connections that might possibly include people who could do that sort of thing.

I waited until the theoretical second hand on my phone made it officially 7:30 before calling Logan. When he answered I said the obligatory, "Oh, I'm sorry, did I get you up?"

"It's Friday. I always sleep in on Friday." Logan didn't sound annoyed, just factual.

"The hard life of a university professor," I teased. "I know, you stayed up late grading papers."

"Don't waste your attempt at humor on me before I've had my coffee."

"Okay, so here's why I called . . ." I gave him the highlights about the break-in, and he immediately suggested we get together to talk about it in more detail. We agreed to meet at the head of the dock in ten minutes. Obviously, he wasn't going to shower.

I put some food in Macavity's bowl and left, too antsy to wait for the full ten minutes. It didn't take Logan the full ten minutes either. On our way to Beth's Café I filled him in on what I knew. While waiting for our orders we guzzled down coffee like it was water and we were stranded in the desert. By the time our food arrived I was hyped up but good.

"They shot the animals," Logan said. Not for the first time.

"They probably considered it an act of mercy."

"I don't think so. It feels to me like they wanted to obliterate Blaine's work."

"Well, if they know that he's dead, and they know what kind of experiments he was doing, then they probably also know that by destroying his lab they will be, at the very least, severely delaying progress on his research. So, I guess I agree."

We took a few minutes to eat, then Logan continued to speculate. "The other possibility is that it's a rival company. And if they have his data, then that puts them—whoever *they* are—in the lead. Or at least it levels the playing field."

"And," I added, "it's also a scary message to anyone who might consider continuing his work."

"Like Bill?"

"Like Bill or anyone else at NorPac."

"Yeah." Logan got thoughtful. "What do you think NorPac's response will be? Throw in the towel? Move the lab to some place safer? Regroup with more security?"

"It's hard to say. They obviously are sensitive to bad publicity or they wouldn't have spun off the research lab as a separate entity and fenced it off like that. Then again, the financial potential if the research succeeds is probably astronomical. So, if I had to guess, they won't disband the research. Maybe move the lab."

"What about Bill?" Logan asked. "He sounded pretty rattled to me."

My phone rang. It was Fiona. I signaled Logan to keep eating while I answered. The first words out of her mouth were,

"Coincidence, hell no. Keep an eye on that bastard, Bryn. Don't trust a thing he says, you hear me?"

"Hey, calm down, Fiona. I doubt I will see him again. But I'm thinking that I ought to give his name to the police. What do you say?"

"Go ahead, but don't expect anything to stick. I'll bet he has a solid alibi for last night."

"Like a woman, you mean?" I laughed. "Well, yes, that's a good possibility.

"If the break-in was as sophisticated as Bill thinks, the police might have some ideas about who is capable of that kind of crime. But it probably also means it will be hard to prove."

Fiona lectured me some more about Keith and his badass connections before telling me she had to run but would be in touch. I sighed as I tapped the hang-up symbol. "Damn," I said. "it's a real shame."

"Don't tell me you're becoming attached to that Scottish gangster."

"Scottish bad boys can be sooo appealing," I reluctantly admitted.

Logan sighed. "Tell me about it." Then he laughed.

"I think there's a story there."

"Youthful fling," he said. Then he frowned. "But take Fiona's advice and stay away from that guy."

"I only had coffee with him, and it didn't sound like he's planning on being back in my life any time soon. So, you needn't worry."

We went our separate ways to get a few things done before Bill called back. Logan went to the university to grade the papers he hadn't managed to complete the night before and to see if any students showed up to talk to him about grades, ideas, or projects they were working on, the typical topics for his office hours. Since it was a beautiful day, he anticipated that most of his students would consider a walk in the Arboretum a higher priority than talking to a professor, so he felt confident he would be able to get away early.

I was slowly making my way through the unruly heap of papers on my desk that I'd put off dealing with, wishing for a distraction, when one came in the form of a knock on my office door. Clients never come to me; I always go to them. Logan raps on the door and then barges in without waiting for a reply. But even if he decided to be polite for once, it couldn't be him, because he was at his office on campus.

"Come in," I yelled. It wasn't a very professional invitation, but I anticipated that it was either my landlord or perhaps another marina tenant.

To my surprise, when the door opened, the person who appeared was someone from my past, my favorite detective, Ben Peterson. We had met the year before over a case he had handled concerning a death at the marina.

"Hi, Bryn," he said, giving me a big smile—white, even teeth flashing like a toothpaste commercial from under the carefully clipped mustache.

I was pleased to see him, but I was surprised. He hadn't called since our one romantic evening together. His lack of follow-up had been both a disappointment and a relief. I really don't like his regulation mustache. On the other hand, he is tall and muscular and has a very pleasant face. He's also good at his job.

"Hi, stranger," I said with a touch of cynicism. "What a surprise." I'm always good at inane remarks when I'm uncomfortable.

He grabbed a chair and pulled it up across from my desk.

"You're looking well," he said. "Like you just got back from vacation."

I laughed. "You're still adept at 'subtle' I see."

"This is an official visit," he admitted. "I volunteered to come by when I saw your name on the list."

"I think I can guess which 'list.'"

"Have you talked with Bill Masters about the break-in?"

"Yes, and he told me he gave the police my name. I assume he told you the reason for my interest in Humanity Health Group."

"Yes, but why don't *you* tell me."

"In my own words?" I teased.

He smiled. "Yes, tell me in your own words about your connection to Jared Blaine and HHG." Then he paused and looked very serious. "As well as your connection to 'Say No to Chimeras.'"

"Wow, the police have been busy. I went to my first meeting just this past week."

"I know."

"Spy? Cameras? Surveillance?"

"You know I can't say."

"Well, if you know all, you know that I've been asked not to return."

"Really?"

"I admitted being in Scotland when Blaine disappeared."

"When you found his body, you mean."

"Well, there isn't a body yet, as far as I know, and the generally accepted story is that he has simply extended his hiking trip. Even though he isn't a hiker, was supposedly in Scotland on business, and now his lab has been broken into." I paused. "So why exactly are you here? It sounds like you have more on your mind than the break-in at HHC."

"I wish it was for pleasure." He sounded like he meant it, and he paused almost wistfully before continuing. "It's true Blaine isn't officially listed as 'missing' yet. But I believe you did come across his body."

"Because you know me, or is there some other reason?"

"In my mind, the pieces don't fit together to justify any other version of reality. And I don't think you would make a mistake about someone being dead." His eyes narrowed as if puzzled by something. "You know, one thing bothers me."

"Only one?" My flippant question sounded lame, even to me.

"Why did you leave the body instead of using your satellite communicator to call for help right away?"

"No one else has questioned that," I said.

"You wouldn't leave without a reason."

I hesitated. "I haven't told anyone this, anyone official, that is."

"You can tell me."

"Will it become part of your report?"

"Why would you hold something back?" he asked instead of answering my question.

"Because the police thought I was off base—in the wrong place or couldn't tell a corpse from a live person. And," I added, "because I was embarrassed. It felt like I had led them on a wild goose chase. But I can assure you what I didn't tell them won't help with your investigation."

"Let me . . ."

". . . be the judge of that," I finished for him.

Reluctantly I told him about feeling like there was someone watching from the trees when I discovered the body. And then later, when the police were convinced that I hadn't discovered a body, it seemed too late to mention that I had been spooked. It also seemed awkward mentioning that I knew that the alleged victim was from Seattle.

"It made it seem like there was some connection between us, when there wasn't. It really was just a coincidence. But the whole situation felt off. And when I got home, I couldn't just forget about Blaine. I felt like I owed it to him to follow up."

"Yes, I imagine that letting the police do their jobs without your help would have been difficult for you," Ben said with an impish grin. Then the detective took over again. "But you need to stay out of this now."

"And just what does that mean?" I felt myself becoming wary.

Ben leaned forward, "These are dangerous people, Bryn. They won't like it if you get in their way."

Detective Peterson had a few more questions for me. Then he left, warning me one last time to stay out of the investigation. But the smile he gave me as he closed the door was neither official nor lacking in warmth. For not the first time I wondered if I could get used to the mustache. Or maybe I could doctor the two sugars he puts in his coffee and shave it off while he slept.

Logan called three times to see if I'd heard from Bill. When I finally couldn't stand it any longer, I called Bill and was surprised when he answered. I'd anticipated getting his voice mail. He told me that the police had kept him busy for hours, then NorPac management had kept him hanging around while they tried to decide what to do, and now all he wanted was to go home, have a drink, and call it a night. When he added that the police hadn't told him anything we hadn't already guessed, I let him off the hook. He promised to keep in touch and let us know what was happening.

Later that evening I joined Logan and Judd on their boat for a drink and some commiseration. The *Carpe Diem* is a comfortable boat inside with plush cushion seating around a wood table. The tabletop is spotless; Judd is fussy about making people use coasters. Both men agreed with Ben that I should stay out of the investigation, but then Logan said he'd go with me to check out the protest demonstration at City Hall the next day. Logan is inconsistent that way. It's one of the things I like about him.

great signs

They were already marching back and forth with their signs in front of City Hall when we arrived, walking in an elongated circle to, as one of their organizers had explained the other night, create a feeling of mass and orderliness. It was also supposed to be a good way to keep the protestors engaged. If participation was random, it was easier for someone to join in or drop out.

I recognized most of the sign holders. Some were wearing "Say No to Chimeras" T-shirts. The T-shirts came in a variety of colors. They had a circle with a line through it superimposed over a monsterish chimera that resembled a demon straight out of Greek mythology. It crossed my mind that the entire scenario would look good on the evening news. And apparently a number of reporters thought the same thing. The event was already being filmed by several local news stations.

I was wearing a hat to hide my red hair and hoped no one would notice me in the crowd that was starting to mill around as if waiting for the show to begin. One of the "Say No" protesters had a megaphone and was leading a chant: "No to chimeras. No to chimeras. No to chimeras." Not exactly catchy, and I overheard a number of bystanders asking, "What's a chimera?"

"Nice signs," Logan commented as we approached.

"Thank you," I said.

"Oh, that's right—your idea."

My idea, yes, and it was definitely the artwork that seemed to be catching the eyes of passersby and reporters. Rather than overtly hostile and homemade, the signs were professional looking and required a second take to get the message.

As I glanced around, I noticed there were two police officers standing to one side. One was talking on his phone. Since I doubted the group had obtained a permit for their small demonstration, my guess was that the officer was calling in for advice and possible back-up. Just in case. The presence of so many reporters suggested that *they* had been clued in about the protest in advance, even if the police hadn't been.

Logan asked if the guy who had threatened me was there, and I pointed him out. In the light of day, he didn't look particularly menacing in his jeans and chimera T-shirt. In fact, the coordinated T-shirts and animal signs somehow made the entire event seem more like a marketing campaign than a protest.

One of the reporters motioned at a protester in a bright green chimera T-shirt and held up a microphone suggestively. The young man eagerly joined the attractive female reporter and smiled as she pushed the microphone at him. The goal was, after all, to get some publicity.

Although I doubted that few, if any, of the people in the growing crowd had the chimera issue on their radar, the demonstration was definitely attracting a lot of interest. Maybe it was having the press there. Or maybe it felt safe to gawk because the sign carriers were in line and the chanting was perfunctory rather than angry. No one was hurling insults at anyone; everything was going smoothly.

Then things suddenly changed.

One minute we were standing there watching a peaceful protest. The next thing I knew, shots had been fired and people were screaming and shoving and running. Before I could react,

Logan grabbed me and pulled me toward a side street. I felt something sting my arm as we moved off. Then we, too, were running. Like stampeded horses with no destination other than "away."

We ran as fast as we could for a couple of blocks. Then Logan herded me toward a line of cars, and we ducked behind them and hunkered down to catch our breath. Another woman wearing a suit and carrying a large leather bag dropped down alongside of us. "Are we safe here?" she asked. "I can't run much further in these shoes."

She was wearing what looked like an expensive pair of snakeskin leather pumps with pointy toes and shiny red soles.

"I'm impressed," I said, "I can't even *walk* in heels that high." Not wanting to insult her, I added, "They're great looking."

She was staring intently at me. "Are you okay?" she asked.

"Yes, why?"

Logan had been peering around the end of the car we were hiding behind, watching the street. When she asked if I was okay, he turned toward me, blinked several times, and said, "Oh my god, you've been shot."

Until that instant I had been blissfully unaware of the blood running down my left arm. As soon as they called attention to it, I felt faint. "How bad is it?" I asked, as if I was disassociated from my own body.

The woman took out her cell phone. "I'll call for an ambulance." she said.

Logan leaned over and examined my arm. "No, that's not necessary. It doesn't look like much. A nick maybe."

"Can you die from a 'nick'?" I asked. I couldn't bear to look at my arm; I had visions of spurting veins and exposed bone.

"Here." The woman reached in her bag and pulled out a silk scarf, a kaleidoscope of colors with fringe on the ends. "Use this," she said, handing it to Logan.

"Oh, I couldn't," Logan protested. It was an attractive scarf, much nicer than anything I had in my closet.

"Yes, you can," I said, starting to panic. "Unless you want to tear up your shirt."

Logan reluctantly took the scarf and wrapped it around my upper arm. My arm was starting to hurt, but not so much that I thought I needed an ambulance. And obviously Logan didn't think there was any urgency. I can read his feelings so easily; if he wasn't worried, then I probably didn't need to be. But, still, I'd been *shot*. It might not be a bad idea to get to a doctor as soon as possible.

"Let's get you back to the car," Logan said. There were sirens screaming in the distance, but there were no more fleeing onlookers in the vicinity. No shots were being fired, nor were there any armed gunmen in sight. Turning to my benefactor he asked, "Want to go with us? I can drop you off somewhere."

"My office is just around the corner. Would you mind walking me there?" She pointed in the direction we would have to go in to get to the car, so it was an easy decision. As we stood up and looked around I half-way expected to hear more shots, but everything was quiet. Unnaturally quiet for a city street.

Logan was solicitous, asking if I felt strong enough to walk and offering to get the car and come back for me. But there was no way I wanted to stay behind on my own.

When we reached the woman's office building, I offered to pay for her scarf. She insisted it wasn't necessary; she was just glad she had been able to help. It occurred to me that she was probably also glad she hadn't been the one shot.

For once we didn't argue over who was going to drive. Logan got a blanket out of the trunk so I wouldn't bleed on my upholstery, and we headed for the ER at the nearest hospital on the hill above the city. On the way we turned on the news to see if we could get an update, but the only coverage was a passing reference to a shoot-out in front of City Hall. Details weren't yet available.

When we arrived at the ER, I expected to see a line of people with gunshot wounds waiting to be treated, but I was apparently the only one so far. The word "gunshot wound" got me immediate attention. But since I was conscious, they made me fill out a bunch of insurance forms and promise them my first-born before they would let me see a doctor, a very young-looking doctor whose name tag said "Dr. Mellon." Not quite Doogie Howser, but close. He motioned me to a narrow cot bed and pulled the curtain around us. Logan had come in with me for moral support. Once I was settled, Dr. Mellon introduced himself. "I'm a resident here, and I've been assigned to take a look at your gunshot wound." It sounded like a line he had just learned to say from a session on how to greet patients. I was adding up the clues: young, resident, just been trained . . . not someone to inspire confidence. So, when Dr. Mellon informed me that he was going to remove the scarf and cut the sleeve off my shirt, I argued with him.

"No way," I said. "No way."

Logan leaned over and explained in a calm voice that the shirt was already ruined. I glanced down at my arm and realized he was right. The shirt was a goner. Reluctantly, I gave in.

After Dr. Mellon unwrapped the scarf, cut away the shirt and finally got a look at my wound he seemed disappointed.

"Looks superficial," he said.

"That's good news, isn't it?" Taking a deep breath, I joined him in looking at my arm. There was blood, *my* blood, seeping out of a dark notch in the side of my arm, not a pretty sight.

"Are you sure it's a gunshot wound?" Dr. Mellon asked. His tone suggested it wasn't nearly that big a deal, maybe a bite from an overzealous spider with large fangs.

"Well, let's put it this way," Logan interrupted. "There was a demonstration interrupted by gunshots, everyone ran away, and then we discovered that Bryn was bleeding." He was obviously irritated with the doctor on my behalf. On the other hand, it seemed to me that he should be pleased that he had been right about the wound being superficial.

"Look," I said as the two men glared at each other. "I don't care what caused it, I just want it taken care of. You can do that, can't you?"

Dr. Mellon blinked as though finally focusing on reality and said, "Of course." Then he added, "Sorry, it's just that I haven't had an opportunity to treat a gunshot wound yet."

"Sorry to disappoint you."

"I didn't mean it like that." He looked somewhat contrite, but not contrite enough to appease Logan.

"Well then?" Logan's tone and nod in the direction of my arm let Dr. Mellon know that he'd better *get on with it.*

Dr. Mellon cleaned my wound, applied some kind of ointment, gave me a prescription for an antibiotic, told me to take Tylenol for pain, and wrote up the incident as a "wound of unknown origins." I guess he wanted his first gunshot case to make better bedtime reading. He might also have figured it wasn't worth reporting to the police and filling out their paperwork. Since I wasn't anxious to hang around, I didn't complain—it was better to be "nicked" by an unknown source than fatally shot.

It was mid-afternoon by the time we got back to the marina. The sun was dancing across the water, leaving sparkling points of light in its wake. Boats were bouncing gently, barely tugging at their lines, like racehorses waiting for the gate to open and the bell to ring. The slight turbulence wasn't the result of wind but of heavy boat traffic, some captains ignoring the "no wake" rule and zipping by as if there wasn't a speed limit.

Logan wanted to walk me to the *Aspara,* but I assured him I was fine, and we parted ways. As I headed down the dock, I passed several boaters whose main reason for owning a boat seemed to be to work on them. Their boats never left the marina. But they were always eager to talk about that boat trip they were going to take *some day.*

Just as I reached the concrete pier where the *Aspara* was tied, Macavity rushed past me, scaring the duck that was sunning itself next to the tall, red planter outside of the small building that had once been an office for the fuel dock and now served as storage space for our landlord. The planter was Hudson's way of trying to class up the pier. Unfortunately, he relied on me to water the plants in it, and I often forgot. It was clear from the way the leaves were drooping that I had been derelict of late. As soon as I've had a nap, I'll get you a drink, I silently promised the thirsty plants as I went by.

Onboard the *Aspara*, Macavity insisted on a treat before he would let me lie down. And he didn't like it when I took his side of the V-berth. But I didn't want to lay on my left side. Nor did I want to face the hull. After making his displeasure known, he curled up alongside me and purred as I stroked his sleek fur. That was the last thing I remembered until I awoke with a start.

The *Aspara* was rocking gently. Had someone stepped aboard? Was that what had awakened me? Friends always made their presence known when they came aboard. But no one was knocking on my hatch or calling my name.

I started worrying about whether the hatch was secure. I couldn't remember whether I'd slid back the bolt or not. Under normal circumstances I might not have been concerned. Sometimes looky-loos come aboard without permission because they don't think anyone cares if they stomp around on your private property. But I'd been shot earlier; I wasn't feeling particularly comfortable with the thought of confronting a stranger, any stranger.

And where was Macavity? He usually announces visitors by pouncing on me when I'm asleep. Maybe he'd already slipped out of his porthole cat door to avoid facing company.

He's not a very social cat.

CHAPTER 14

"who's there?"

A lot of boaters have guns aboard. You never know who or what you might encounter traveling in some isolated location. From time to time I've considered getting a gun, but I've never followed through. Nor did I have any other kind of weapon at hand. Not that I thought I needed a weapon. Unless someone really was trying to break into my boat.

Suddenly, an idea that had been at the back of my mind all along, suppressed by fear and denial, leapt to the forefront. What if I had been a specific target at the demonstration? What if someone had been aiming at me and I had turned away at just the right moment? And what if that same person had come to my boat to finish the job? It seemed farfetched, but if even remotely possible, I couldn't just stay in my bunk hoping my fears were unfounded. I had to do something.

As I sat up, I heard the hatch rattle softly. Someone was on board and definitely *trying* to get in. I hurried into the main salon and looked around for a makeshift weapon. There was a knife laying on the table, but I couldn't make myself pick it up. I saw that the bolt was secured, so I didn't need to panic, just get prepared. The cast iron frypan my mother had given me was on the stove. That would have to do. I grabbed it and moved toward the hatch.

Should I wait until someone actually managed to break in? Or should I let them know that I knew they were out there and act as though I was prepared to defend myself? I picked up my cell and dialed Logan's number. When he answered I called out, "Who's there?" for the benefit of Logan and the potential intruder.

The rattling stopped.

"I know someone is there," I yelled. "Either tell me who you are or I'm calling the police." No, I thought, that wasn't the right thing to say. There's no either-or negotiating with someone who wants to harm you. "I'm calling them right now," I shouted.

Logan was yelling something, and I could hear him panting. Undoubtedly, he was already making a beeline for my boat. The consequences of what I had done by calling him suddenly hit me. If there was a dangerous person out there, what could Logan do? "Don't come, Logan," I whispered into the phone with my hand over my mouth. "They could be armed. Just call the police."

"Coming, Bryn," I heard him say.

"*No*, don't," I said louder. "Call the police."

I felt someone step off the boat, causing it to rock unnaturally.

"Logan," I screamed into my phone. "Call the police. Stay away from the *Aspara*!" I was frantic now. What if by calling Logan I got him shot? I would never be able to live with myself.

Still clutching the frypan, I pulled back the bolt and pushed the hatch open. Then I climbed out into the cockpit and peeked out from under the tarp that covers the aft deck. I was surprised to find it was dark outside. I must have slept longer than I'd thought.

There was no one there. "*Logan*," I yelled into the phone again. "Can you hear me?!"

"Bryn, I'm on my way."

"N*ooo*. Stop! Stop right now!"

Apparently, he finally registered what I'd been saying. "Why?" he asked, sounding out of breath.

"Do you see anyone on the dock? If you do, get out of sight. Right now. They could be armed."

For a few seconds Logan didn't say anything. I put down the fry pan and climbed out on the pier. Then I went behind the small square building and looked around the corner to check the dock for the intruder. There's a light on a pole at the end of the dock. I just caught a glimpse of someone pass under the light and head for the steps when Logan came back on the line.

"Bryn, are you okay?"

"Yes. Are you?"

"Yes. But I feel as though I should have tried to stop him."

"Did you get a look at the guy?"

"Barely. The dock isn't very well lit. And I was trying to stay out of sight on one of the finger floats."

I saw Logan coming in my direction and went to meet him.

"Let's go back to the *Carpe Diem*," he said. "We can wait for the police there."

"I haven't called them yet. Since nothing actually happened, do you think I should?"

"I don't know, Bryn. First someone shoots you, now this. I think you need to report it."

Just then, Judd, Logan's partner, appeared at the top of the steps carrying a large pizza box. "Hey, you two," he called down to us. "What's happening?" He sounded friendly, not worried.

Logan and I exchanged glances. Since Judd is a lawyer and much more conservative overall than Logan, we both knew what his response would be to the situation. "Have you told him about the demonstration and me getting shot?" I whispered.

"Not really," Logan whispered back. "He got in late last night from a business trip and has been at the office today. I was going to tell him this evening. Let me take the lead, okay?"

We met Judd at the bottom of the steps. "That smells good," Logan said. He turned toward me, "Want to watch us eat it?"

Judd shook his head. "We have salad and bread too, more than enough for three."

"Great, I haven't eaten yet," I said. Since I didn't want to be alone, I might as well take advantage of the offer of food. "By the way," I added. "You didn't happen to see a car driving away, did you?"

"Just now?" Judd thought about it. "Yeah, a dark Ford. Why?"

"Did you see who was driving?" Logan asked, sounding a bit too eager.

"It was too dark to see much." Judd eyed us suspiciously.

"You two up to something?"

"It's a long story," I said.

"It usually is," Judd commented with a tinge of sarcasm.

"Actually, I could use your advice," I said. Judd is very level-headed and has a way of cutting to the heart of issues, quickly and concisely. Not that he always tells me what I want to hear. But I respect his opinion.

Logan walked me back to the *Aspara* so I could lock up before heading to the *Carpe Diem*. It took a sizeable helping of salad, two slices of pizza and several glasses of wine for me to bring Judd up to speed. Since Judd had been out of town Logan hadn't told him much about my trip or what had happened since. I started from the beginning with the discovery of the body. From there I explained what Logan and I had learned about Blaine's research and how I had become involved with the protestors. I could tell Judd wasn't happy about us attending the protest after I had been warned off, but he refrained from making comments and only interrupted to ask occasional questions for clarification.

Although Judd's specialty is contract law, he finds all aspects of the law interesting and is very well read. That's why I thought he would have some sage advice on what we should do next. But I have to admit he surprised me. "Don't you have a friend who's a police officer?" he asked.

"Not exactly. I mean, I know a detective, but he has already suggested I avoid getting involved. So . . ."

"So, he's a sensible guy," Judd finished for me with a touch of sarcasm. "But I would ask him for guidance on this. He might be able to do something unofficial."

"In other words, you don't think I should call the police about the break-in attempt?"

"Oh, I think you should report it, but I don't see what they can do. You may be up to your eyeballs in some serious shit."

Serious *shit*? That didn't sound like legalese. "What do you mean?"

"For one thing, these protesters you've got yourself mixed up with . . ." I opened my mouth to interrupt, but he motioned for me to wait. ". . . they have been involved in several serious incidents over the years. You may remember a lab that was set on fire where someone died."

"You mean the that time where they set the animals loose?" Logan asked.

"Yeah. And it's not as though it did the animals any favors. I don't think there were many happy endings, if any."

"What happened?" I asked. I only vaguely remembered reading about it.

"Well, one of the scientists went inside to retrieve his laptop and didn't make it back out. As for the freed animals, several were hit by cars. Some died because they couldn't take care of themselves, couldn't find food or water. Only a few survived. They were eventually rounded up and returned to the lab. The whole thing was a disaster."

"They seem like such committed people," I said. "I mean the ones I've met seem to be concerned about animal welfare, and they make some good points about the potential negative consequences of Blaine's research. The issues at least deserve an open discussion."

"Oh, I agree," Judd said. "But groups like these attract crazies as well as people with honest concerns. That's the problem."

I knew he had a point, and I also agreed that I should call the police as well as Ben. Although all I really wanted to do was have another glass of wine and forget all about Jared Blaine and everything that had happened since I'd returned from Scotland. But I knew that neither Logan nor Judd would let me off the hook. "And," Judd concluded, "I hate to say this, but I think you should raft the *Aspara* next to the *Carpe Diem* this evening." He paused. "Just keep that annoying cat of yours away."

Logan went with me to move my boat. Macavity still wasn't around. He would either find the new location or be very angry with me tomorrow. I just hoped he was okay.

Once the *Aspara* was rafted to the *Carpe Diem*, I called the police to report the attempted break-in. They asked a few questions, including whether I wanted someone to come by to take a look, but I said it wasn't necessary. Then I called Ben. He wasn't available, so I left a message giving him a brief overview of what had happened, explaining that I had reported the incident but would welcome any suggestions he might have.

Although I thought I would never fall asleep given the events of the day, I was exhausted. The minute my head hit the pillow I was out.

CHAPTER 15

skewered

In my dream I was inside a red Honda trapped in a junkyard car crusher. Why a red Honda, I have no idea. But I could feel the pressure on my chest as I was slowly being compressed. I tried to cry out, but all I could manage was a muffled, "Ugh."

Puurrrr.

"Ugh," I said again.

Puurrrr. A rough tongue licked my chin.

That woke me up. "Macavity. Yuk." I wiped my chin. He isn't usually a licker. Then it hit me. I wasn't being crushed. And Macavity was safe. I reached out to give him a hug, but he was too quick for me. Niceties were over. I had moved his home without telling him, and it was time for a hearty breakfast to make up for it.

I barely had time to feed Macavity, make myself some coffee and get dressed before the frogs started partying. It was Ben returning my call. I gave him a few more details about what had happened and asked if we could meet face-to-face so I could get his perspective and advice on what I should do. He said that he could be at my office in a half hour.

There was no one stirring on the *Carpe Diem*, so after finishing my coffee, I tacked a note on their door telling them

94

where I had gone and headed down the dock. The sky was overcast; it looked like rain. People with lawns and gardens were probably pleased at the prospect, but living on a boat, what I longed for was one sunny day after another. With a little wind thrown in for good sailing.

When I found the door to my office unlocked, my first thought was that I had failed to lock it the last time I was there. I've been known to do that before. My next thought was that maybe I'd been robbed. I quickly pushed the door open and was relieved to see my computer right where I'd left it. It's the main thing of value in my office, and even though I am good about backing up all of my information, I would hate to have to go to the bother of replacing it.

I was just breathing a sigh of relief when I noticed that my dagger letter opener was perpendicular to my desk, handle up. It took me a moment to take in the entire scenario.

Bubbles III was impaled on my wood desk. The pointy blade had pierced his tiny body and was embedded in the once smooth wooden surface.

The appropriate feeling would have been to feel compassion for Bubbles' unfortunate demise. But instead, all I could think was, why me? Now I would have to buy still another goldfish.

The scene before me was just starting to sink in when I heard movement behind me. I reacted quickly, leaping aside and preparing for an attack.

"Hey, take it easy," a familiar voice said.

I not only relaxed, I went weak-kneed, almost collapsing. Ben reached out to steady me. He was early. But too late to save my goldfish.

"You okay?" he asked. Then his eyes landed on Bubbles' body, a tiny golden corpse amidst the stacks of papers and file folders on my desk. "What the . . .?" He let go of my arm and went over to inspect Bubbles' remains. "Who did this?" he asked.

"Someone who doesn't like goldfish," I offered.

Ben looked around my messy office as if trying to decide

whether this was its normal state or if it had been tossed. "Anything else, ah, tampered with?" he asked.

I took a deep breath and tried to focus on the state of my office. "Well, they didn't take my computer, and it doesn't look like they've messed with my papers." Except for Bubbles pinned to my desk, my messy office looked normal.

I went over to my computer and logged on. The request for my password came up. "Unless they figured out my password, they didn't access any of my files." Not that I could imagine anyone caring about the files on my computer.

"I assume this has something to do with what you called me about."

"Unless there really is someone out there who hates goldfish." I always get flip when I'm upset.

Ben did not look amused. "Okay," he said, "you'd better start from the beginning." He looked around for a place to sit down.

I stood there, still trying to assess how I felt and why someone had done this. It was just a fish, but the act of desecration made me feel vulnerable. And frightened. Probably the reaction they wanted. It was almost worse than being shot at.

"Can we go somewhere else?" I asked. I couldn't take my eyes off the fishbowl with its layer of colored pebbles on the bottom, the miniature lava rock pass-through and limp strand of seaweed. Home of the late Bubbles III, now skewered by my letter opener.

"Oh, sorry. Of course. Why don't you wait outside while I take a few pictures. Then let's go to that coffee shop across the street."

What had once seemed like a promising relationship with Ben had fizzled out. But we hadn't actually had a break-up; more like a stumble at the starting gate. So, there was no particular awkwardness. Just missed opportunity. And under the circumstances, it felt good to have someone there who was both official and a sort-of friend.

Once we had coffee in front of us, I gave him the full story about the attempted break-in, confessed my fears about being targeted at the demonstration, and asked for his advice. "Well, we don't know what they would have done if they had succeeded in breaking into your boat. But it looks like the break-in of your office was intended to frighten you off."

"If they're trying to scare me, they're doing a good job," I said.

Ben rotated the coffee cup in his hands. "If it weren't for you getting shot at . . ." He paused. "Tell me again what happened at the demonstration when the shooting started."

I went through it again, the few seconds it takes to register that the sound you are hearing is a gun being fired, Logan's quick reaction to what was happening, him grabbing me and pulling me away from the crowd toward the side street. Then running until we needed to catch our breath, hiding behind a row of cars, and the woman who noticed I was bleeding.

"So, if Logan hadn't pulled you away, if you had remained standing where you were, where would the bullet have hit you?" As soon as he asked the question, I could tell he regretted it. He was undoubtedly reacting to the look on my face. Even though I couldn't see myself, if my expression matched the shock I was feeling, it wasn't a pretty sight. Somehow, until that moment, I hadn't thought much about that "what if" scenario. I had concluded that the shot had either been a random hit, or, if aimed at me, a warning. Although the details of who and why had remained elusive. The possibility that someone may have tried to do away with me altogether changed everything. Ben reached over and placed his hand on mine. "A dead goldfish is one thing," he said. "Being shot at is a very serious matter."

"But why would they ruin their own demonstration by shooting at me? That doesn't make sense, does it? They would have had lots of other opportunities. Isn't it more likely that it was just my bad luck to be standing there when the shooting started?" I desperately wanted his reassurance.

"It strikes me as significant that no other injuries were reported."

"I haven't heard anything about the shooter or shooters being identified or caught yet. It could have been a an attempt to stop the demonstration and discourage the group against protesting in the future."

"You're right, it could have been. I'm not sure what to think. But my advice to you is to lay low for a while. Avoid contact with the 'Say No to Chimeras' group. Don't talk to anyone involved with Jared Blaine. Don't go out alone at night. And consider taking a vacation."

"I just got back from a vacation. That's what started all of this."

"Look, Bryn, I know how stubborn you can be . . ."

I wanted to interrupt and tell him he had no idea just how stubborn I could be. And I didn't think he knew me well enough to make such a judgment in the first place.

". . . but in this instance, brains are no match for someone determined to come after you."

"But how determined can they be?" I countered. "I mean, I don't know anything, and I'm certainly not in a position to get in anyone's way. Whatever it is that they're up to."

"You've obviously done something. Or they think you know something you shouldn't. You've hit a nerve. The bottom line is that you need to play it safe. Don't do any more snooping around. If Blaine's dead, let the police do their job."

"Snooping around?" I echoed, not pleased with the characterization of what I'd been doing.

For a moment he looked puzzled by my response, then he said, "I didn't mean it like that."

"So how *did* you mean it?" I knew he was trying to be helpful, but I didn't like seeing myself through his eyes. It felt like he was branding me as an incompetent amateur.

He sighed. "I don't want to argue with you, Bryn; I want to help. And most of all, I don't want to see you get hurt."

Reluctantly, I tried to be gracious. "I know. And I appreciate you taking the time to talk with me about this." But I am *not* a snoop, I added silently. I just don't like to leave puzzles unsolved.

On the way back to the marina he told me he was going to send someone over to check for prints on the letter opener and suggested that I stay away from my office until the evidence was removed. He also admitted that he'd be surprised if any prints were found. Then, probably to appease me, he promised that if he learned anything specific about the shooting at the demonstration, he would let me know immediately. He left me at the parking area above the marina with one last comment about how he would be checking in with me on a regular basis, adding that I should feel free to call him any time day or night.

Knowing that Ben was there if I needed him made me feel a little better about things. Not a whole lot, but a little. I would have felt even better knowing who was after me and how serious they were about wanting me to butt out of whatever it was I was butting into.

I was just starting down the stairs from the parking lot when Logan came bursting out of my office. When he saw me he yelled, "Where have you been?!"

"Ben came by," I explained. Before I could continue, Logan interrupted.

"The fish, what happened to your fish?" He was very excited.

"He's dead," I explained.

"I could see that." Now Logan seemed angry. "Your note said you'd be in your office, and when you didn't answer . . . and then I saw the fish . . ."

I reached over and gave Logan a hug. "I'm sorry, I should have called when I went for coffee with Ben. But I was upset too."

Logan hugged me back. Then he pulled away and asked, "Who did that to, ah, Bubbles?"

"Someone who wanted to send a message," I acknowledged. Message received.

surprise!

The last thing I wanted to do was have dinner with my family. But I had promised. My mother can be overbearing at times, convinced I'm wasting my life because I'm still single. My father, on the other hand, has always been supportive. If not in front of my mother, then discreetly behind her back. His only sin in my eyes was agreeing to name me Bryn Geneva Baczek.

Geneva was my grandmother's name. My mother had also chosen a Welsh first name for my brother, Dylan, but he was lucky enough to have a grandfather named Michael. So, he is Dylan Michael. But we share an unpronounceable last name.

I never dress up for Sunday dinner, partly to irritate my mother and partly to enjoy the look of disapproval from my brother's second wife, Angelina. He calls her "Angel," a bit too saccharine for my less sentimental tastes, but I try to be under-standing. Well, maybe not all the time. But I work at maintaining a good relationship with them for the sake of their twins, Noah and Emma, age five. I adore them and spoil them, and they in turn adore me. It's a good arrangement. And that's why I keep replacing Bubbles. For Emma's sake. But I look forward to the day when she reaches an age when it doesn't matter anymore, and I can flush my very last goldfish.

Today I was wearing a pair of jeans that had some tacky embroidery on the sides of each leg and strategic holes in both knees. I'd picked them up cheap at a consignment shop. But it was the baggy T-shirt that I knew would result in raised eyebrows. It was bright yellow and had a picture of a chicken crossing the road with the caption: *I dream of a world where chickens can cross the road without having their motives questioned.* It had been a gift from Catrin, Dylan's oldest daughter from his first marriage. She is the only one excused from the mandatory requirement to attend Sunday dinners, although she comes when she feels like it. Why my mother lets her off the hook I'm not sure. I just wish I could manage it from time to time without declaring war.

Everyone was already there when I arrived carrying a huge bag with my presents from Scotland. I ran into Angelina in the hall and she gave me a onceover and did the thing she does with her mouth to indicate disapproval. My mother wasn't quite as discreet. "Yellow is *not* your color," she said instead of, "Hello, my favorite daughter is here." Then she smiled, and, ignoring the bag I was carrying, took my arm and said, "We have a surprise for you."

I wasn't sure I liked the sound of that, but it was too late to escape, so I let her lead me into the dining room. And when I saw who was there, I was definitely surprised. Surprised, shocked, bewildered, and mad. I felt a jolt of energy course through my body as I struggled with competing emotions.

"Keith," I said, biting back my instinctive desire to follow saying his name by expressing out loud the thought that was bouncing around in my head: *What the hell are you doing in my parents' house?*

Keith came around the end of the table, put his hands on my shoulders and pulled me toward him for a brotherly peck on the cheek. "I bet you're surprised to see me here," he said in his smooth Scottish brogue.

My mother was beaming at us, clearly taken in by Keith's charm. The rest of the family was gawking, obviously curious to learn more about this unexpected and attractive guest. Catrin was staring at him as if he was a movie star and she was his biggest fan, obviously pleased with herself that she'd chosen to come to dinner today. Noah and Emma were hanging back, waiting to see what was going to happen next.

Mother announced that we should all sit down because dinner was about to be served. I smiled inanely at everyone, sat my bag of goodies on the floor and hurried after her into the kitchen.

As soon as we were out of earshot, I asked, "What's he doing here?"

"Bryn, I thought you'd be pleased." She seemed truly puzzled by my reaction.

"Did he just show up on your doorstep?" I asked.

"Well, yes, as a matter of fact." She was busy putting bowls of food on trays. "You can take that one in," she said.

I was not to be put off. "But why did you invite him to dinner?"

She paused. "He explained that he had met you in Scotland and was trying to get in touch. I thought since you would be here shortly, and there's always more than enough food . . ." She left the thought hanging. "Is there a problem?"

There *was*. But I didn't want to involve my parents. It seemed as though I had no choice but to go along with the charade. "No, Mother, no problem. I'm just surprised, that's all." I picked up a tray and headed for the dining room.

When I entered the dining room with the tray of food, I caught Emma and Noah poking through the presents in the bag I had left on the floor. You can always count on them to lighten the mood. "Yes," I said to their unasked question, "there are a few things in there for you."

"There're no names," Noah complained.

"That's so no one gets nosey when they shouldn't." I grabbed his nose and pretended to twist it. He howled with fake pain. "After dinner we'll open them, okay?" They both made faces at the enforced wait but responded obediently to their father's suggestion that they take their seats. Dylan and I have an uneasy sibling relationship, but I appreciate the fact that he is a good father.

"It smells delicious," Keith said enthusiastically. My mother looked as pleased as if he had presented her with a gourmet cook of the year award.

The food was a flashback to my childhood. The centerpiece was a spiral ham on a large white platter. There were mashed sweet potatoes with coconut-pecan topping, green beans, rolls and salad. It wasn't one of my mother's fancy meals, but it instantly brought back happy memories.

My father picked up a sharp knife and long fork to ritualistically cut pieces of ham to be passed around on a smaller white platter. Dinner was officially under way.

Throughout dinner Keith more than held up his end of the conversation. He went out of his way to charm everyone, using his brogue and his dimple to maximum advantage. His description about how he had saved me from a swarm of midges in the car park sounded noble and romantic. Emma and Noah seemed particularly taken with him, especially when he told them a story about Nessie that made them gasp in awe.

He was vague and playfully mysterious when I asked him directly how he had come up with my parents' address. His good-natured evasiveness made it seem like he was interested in pursuing a relationship with me and that I needed to be cajoled into it. I kept racking my brain to remember if I'd said something about our Sunday dinners to him. Or was it just another *coincidence* that his timing was so good?

After dinner Dylan and I helped with the clean-up while Angelina, Catrin and my father entertained the twins and our guest. I felt betrayed when Noah and Emma happily went off with Keith as if he was a long-lost uncle.

"So, what's the story?" Dylan asked me as he put plates into the dish washer.

"No story," I said somewhat abruptly.

"What? A handsome Scotsman shows up on your doorstep and there's no 'story'?"

"Not *my* doorstep. And no story."

"I think he's delightful," mother interposed.

"Emma and Noah certainly like him," Dylan observed.

"I didn't invite him. And you won't be seeing him again," I added a bit too emphatically.

"Why?" Both Dylan and my mother had stopped what they were doing and were staring at me.

"Because he's . . . he's . . . a con man." There, maybe that would satisfy them.

"What does that mean?" mother asked.

"It means that he's good at getting people to like him, but he has a shady background."

Mother dismissed my comment with a wave of her dishcloth. "I think you should give him a chance." Then she turned back to the dishes.

Dylan rolled his eyes. I made a face at him. It was like we'd reverted to our twelve-year-old selves. It didn't take much when we were back in our parents' house.

Noah was sitting on Keith's lap when we rejoined everyone in the living room. Emma was seated at his feet. He was teaching them a Scottish song. I felt somewhat triumphant when I picked up the bag of presents and captured their attention.

Normally I only buy presents for Noah and Emma when I travel, but since I had spent so much time in towns, I had gotten carried away. There was something for everyone in the family. I had Noah and Emma hand out the gifts, saving theirs until last. Father got a tartan cashmere scarf that I knew he would like but never wear. My mother loves pins, so her gift was a lovely Celtic weave brooch. There was a bottle of malt whiskey for Dylan, a pair of Celtic drop earrings with tiny green stones for Catrin, and a box of chocolates from Cocoa Mountain for Angelina. Angelina would probably think I bought candy for her to ruin her trim figure, but it was actually an act of desperation because I couldn't think of anything else and didn't want to leave her out.

Finally, Emma and Noah got to open their gifts. Emma instantly loved her black watch tartan kilt and giant stuffed Nessie. Noah gave his Celtic dragon T-shirt a brief nod before focusing on his junior playable bagpipe. He loves music, although I was fairly certain that wouldn't be what he produced with those bagpipes. Out of the corner of my eye I saw Dylan and Angelina exchange looks. I mentally gave myself a pat on the back.

After the gifts were distributed, I got Keith's attention and nodded toward the door. He quickly took the hint, and we said our goodbyes. Everyone seemed sad to see Keith leave. Once outside, I let it rip. "You had no right to come here," I began.

"Hold on," he said, putting his hands in the air. "I come in peace." He gave me one of his lovely smiles. But I wasn't buying.

"Look, I don't know what you're up to, but . . ." I hesitated. Maybe it wasn't a good idea to tip my hand.

"Can't I just be here because I wanted to see you again?"

"I thought you said you were here on business."

"I am. But there's nothing wrong with mixing business and pleasure, is there?"

"But why come to my parents' house?"

"Your boat wasn't in its slip, and it was easy to locate your parents. It helps to have a distinctive name like Baczek." With his Scottish accent his pronunciation didn't sound anything like my last name, but I didn't bother to correct him. I didn't intend to give him an opportunity to say it again. Meanwhile, my brain was screaming that he knew where I lived; he'd been to the marina. Could he have been responsible for Bubbles' demise? If so, why?

"So, when are you returning to Scotland?" I made an effort to keep my tone civil.

He laughed. "That doesn't sound like you want me to hang around."

"Did you stop by my office?" I asked, abruptly changing the subject. Hoping to take him by surprise.

"No, I didn't know you had an office. Where is it?" We'd been standing next to my car while we talked. I didn't know what he expected to do next, but I knew what I wanted to do—get as far away from him as possible. So I said I needed to run; I was meeting someone for drinks. He didn't protest. He simply smiled and said, "Our paths may cross again." A promise or a warning?

I called Sophie and asked her to meet me at our usual place, in the bar. She suggested I stop by her place, but I didn't want to do that. If Keith followed me, I didn't want to lead him to her. Finally, she agreed. Twenty minutes later we were ordering wine, and I was getting ready to unload. By our second glass of wine we had analyzed Keith up and down, right to left, and all around. But we couldn't make sense of his visit.

"If he wants to warn you off," Sophie said, "he shouldn't be quite so subtle."

"Killing Bubbles wasn't subtle."

"But you don't know it was him."

We'd already gone over this ground, several times, so there wasn't much more to say. There was no way I could attribute anything that had happened to Keith, but he always seemed to pop up when something bad occurred.

Sophie sighed. "If he's as handsome as you say he is, maybe you shouldn't have brushed him off."

"What am I supposed to do—pretend to be flattered by his attention?"

"Well, this way you don't have the pleasure of his company, and you don't have any way of finding out more about his intentions, whatever they might be."

It was my turn to sigh. "You're probably right."

"There's no 'probably' about it"

"So, he knows I don't trust him, and I won't have an opportunity to inveigle the truth out of him."

Sophie giggled.

"What's so funny?"

"You. *Inveigling* the truth out of a handsome kilt wearing

Scot. I assume that involves some undercover work?" She giggled some more.

"That's it," I said. "No more wine for you." I poured what remained in the bottle into my glass.

"No fair," she said.

"Life isn't fair."

"I think I read that on a bathroom wall recently."

"You probably read 'life sucks.'"

"That's it. Life sucks."

"Ain't that the truth." With that, we finished off our wine, ordered two coffees, and tried for one last time to make sense of everything that had happened recently. We didn't succeed, but we finally felt sober enough to drive ourselves home.

I called Logan from the marina parking lot and asked him to come and meet me. There didn't seem to be anyone around, but then, if there *was* someone lurking in the shadows, they would hardly reveal themselves before it was too late to take evasive action. Just to be safe, I had my pepper spray in hand as I started down the stairs. Logan showed up before I was halfway down. Together we made our way along the dimly lit dock with its dark corners and gently rocking boats.

Since I didn't have to drive again that evening, I gladly accepted Logan's offer of a glass of wine as an excuse to spend some time with them before returning to the *Aspara*. Judd and he had just finished a late dinner and were settling in for the evening. I entertained them with the story of the Sunday family dinner and the surprise guest. Both men agreed that Keith was up to no good. They even considered the possibility that he'd been the shooter at the demonstration. At the very least they were convinced he was responsible for Bubbles' untimely death. What none of us could figure out was *why*. The little dots refused to connect or be forced into a pattern like the standard uniformity of polka dots on women's apparel. They remained totally random, free-form facts that defied logic.

That night I fell asleep picturing Keith grinning like Jack

Nicholson in *The Shining* as he held Bubbles down and stabbed him through the midsection.

CHAPTER 17

understatement

I t took me several cups of coffee to brace myself to go to my office the next morning. When I arrived, there was a note pinned to the door. It was from Hudson, my landlord. He wanted me to come see him right away. I had a few files that I wanted to drop off in my office first, but my key didn't seem to be working. I was still struggling with it when a shadow fell across the doorway.

"Bryn, I wanted to warn you," Hudson said over my shoulder.

I turned toward him. He was holding a plastic bag filled with water. Inside a tiny goldfish flopped around. "Bubbles IV?" I asked.

"Yes, I talked with the officer. He told me about what happened." Hudson held out the new Bubbles. "I'm so sorry. It must have been distressing."

I accepted the gift; but at the same time, I couldn't help but feel that I would be better off with a pit bull.

"You may have noticed that your key doesn't work anymore." Hudson motioned toward my office door. "That's why I left the note. I had the locks changed."

It was then I noticed that my office door now had two locking mechanisms.

"And I added a deadbolt." He reached into his pocket and handed me two keys on a metal ring.

"Thank you," I said, juggling the file folders and the keys in my left hand. "I appreciate it." Not that I thought it would keep anyone out. But it was a kind gesture.

Hudson stood there as if trying to think of what else he should say. His formality, slightly stooped shoulders and greying hair make him seem older than he actually is. And although I've known him a fairly long time, I don't feel like I really know him. I still think of him as my landlord rather than as a friend.

"I just wanted to say that, well, if there's anything you need . . ."

"I'm fine, Hudson." I wasn't entirely certain that was true, but it seemed like the right thing to say in response to his concern.

Since I had my hands full with Bubbles IV and the files I'd brought with me, I asked Hudson if he would mind doing the honors. He took the keys back from me, unlocked the door and held it open as I slipped inside. He followed me in and placed my new set of keys on the edge of my desk. Then he said goodbye, closing the door firmly behind him. After he was gone, I stood there for a few minutes trying to recapture the positive feelings I've always had about my office.

The body had been removed, but there remained a narrow slit in my desk where the dagger had penetrated the wood. I wasn't sure whether I could fill the gap and have it blend with the rest of the desk top, but I knew I would have to try. Maybe I could put something there to permanently hide the blemish.

What that would be I wasn't sure. Maybe a business card holder or a box for office supplies, something, anything.

As a temporary measure, I laid the files I'd brought with me over the spot on my desk while I introduced Bubbles IV to his new home. I just hoped the ghosts of the many past residents didn't haunt the bowl. I really did need to purchase something to change the look of it. Not for Bubbles, but for me. Maybe I could even buy a bigger bowl, one with a different shape, one that didn't serve as a constant reminder of the fate of Bubbles III.

Before I'd had time to do more than open the first folder there was a knock on the door. A polite, timid knock. Not one I recognized. With my pepper spray in hand, I opened the door a crack and peeked out. A well-dressed couple, both in their early sixties, stood there. And although they didn't look particularly happy, they didn't look menacing either. I slipped the pepper spray in my pocket and opened the door about halfway.

"Are you Bryn *Backzeck*?" the man asked.

Although they were a little off on the pronunciation, they were clearly referring to me. "Yes, and you are?"

"Could we come in, please?" the woman said.

I couldn't think of any reason to say "no," so I opened the door, and motioned them inside. He looked around and saw the extra folding chair I keep propped against the bookshelf in the corner and went over and got it while the woman sat down in the chair across from my desk. I took a seat behind my desk and waited for them to say something. Somehow, I didn't think they were going to be clients.

"I'm John Blaine," the man said as he sat down. "And this is my wife, Marie." She nodded. "We're here to talk to you about our son, Jared."

I was stunned. And for once, speechless. Was I supposed to say I was sorry for their loss? Or did they think he was still on vacation? And what in the hell were they doing in my office?

"Ah, how can I help you?" I asked.

The two looked at each other. Marie Blaine took a deep breath and said, "I understand you have something that belongs to our son." They both waited expectantly for me to respond.

"What makes you think that?" I didn't have a clue what they were talking about.

"Either our son's cell phone isn't working or he's outside of a service area. Anyway, we've asked the police to try and find him. They suggested we talk with you about what's missing."

"But what would make the police think I have something of his?" And why on earth would they have given the couple my name?

"We just know what they told us," John Blaine said. "Now if you would be so kind . . ."

"I'm really sorry, but I'm afraid I, ah, only met your son briefly. And he didn't give me anything." Before I could ask what it was they thought I had, John Blaine learned forward across my desk.

"Maybe you *took* something from him," he said in an accusing tone.

"No, I didn't," I said firmly. "What is it you think I might have?"

They exchanged looks again before he responded. "You took something from his backpack, and you know it." Now he sounded angry, and his wife's face had turned a mottled red. "And we want you to return his property to us."

I stood up to give myself some authority and to indicate the conversation was over. "As I said, I'm sorry your son is, ah, out of reach, but I can't help you. I don't know where he is, and I certainly don't have anything that belongs to him."

They continued sitting there as if they were going to refuse to leave until they got what they had come for.

"Do you mind telling me the name of the police officer who sent you to me?" I asked. "Maybe we can get him or her on the telephone and clear this up."

The two exchanged still another look and simultaneously stood up. Then, without a word, they headed for the door. Mrs. Blaine in the lead, her husband right behind her. He paused in the doorway and said over his shoulder, "We'll be back. If you know what's good for you, you'll give us what we want."

"But I don't have anything . . .," I said to their retreating backs.

As he slammed my door shut, the wobbly stand in the corner wobbled, the shelves rattled, the water in the fishbowl sloshed, and I collapsed onto my desk chair. The exchange had been both upsetting and strange. Why wouldn't Jared's parents tell me what they thought I'd removed from their son's backpack? And what made them think I'd taken anything in the first place? I had told the rescue team and the police that I had looked in the outer pocket of his pack to see who he was, so I suppose it wasn't a huge leap to assume that I had looked through the rest of the pack as well. But why were his parents so upset? Why had they threatened me? Did they think their son's missing computer had been in the backpack? If so, why didn't they just ask if I had his computer? There was something very odd about the entire situation.

The longer I thought about it, the stranger it seemed. It crossed my mind that maybe the couple hadn't even been Jared Blaine's parents. Maybe they were connected to the killer or to the "Say No" group. Just another ploy to get me to give up the missing data that I didn't have.

It was just after 8:00 p.m. in Scotland, so I thought I had a good chance of getting through to Fiona. When she didn't answer I left a message and asked her to call me as soon as possible. I wanted to know who had given the Blaines my name and location. Hopefully Fiona could help me verify whether a Scottish official had talked to someone claiming to be one of Jared's parents. And if not, and if the Blaines were legit, then who gave them that information? But if not an official, then who?

I sat there trying to get my brain to come up with plausible answers to half-formed questions, but nothing was clicking. My eyes started scanning the books on my shelf. Familiar books, familiar titles, not neatly categorized but . . . Then it hit me— something wasn't right. I had the bad habit of putting books back helter-skelter. But now they were mostly lined up properly, as if a librarian had come by and tidied up. You could clearly read the titles of each book.

After the break-in in which Bubbles III met his demise, I had done an inventory to make certain nothing was missing. But I hadn't thought about the possibility that someone had searched my office looking for something that wasn't there.

I started scrutinizing everything, wishing I were more systematic about how I stored things so I could tell more precisely what had been moved. My drawers were a mess, so I had no way of telling whether they'd been searched. There were no rugs to look under. No hidden compartments. No plants. But someone had gone through my books. They had to have been looking for something small, something that would go in or behind a book. Not a laptop, maybe a tablet. A thumb drive perhaps? Unless they were just doing a random search.

Had Jared's parents, or the people claiming to be them, already looked through my office for whatever it was they believed I had taken from their son? After failing to find what they were after, had they then decided to try the straightforward approach and demand that I return the mysterious object? If so, why wouldn't they tell me what it was they thought I had taken? And although I could imagine the two of them going through my office searching for whatever it was they wanted, I somehow couldn't make the leap to either of them being responsible for taking Bubbles' life.

There was another knock on my door, neither timid nor bold. Just a middling "are you in there" sort of knock. Even so, I was half afraid to answer. Although I told myself that someone up to no good wouldn't bother knocking. Still, this time I asked, "Who's there?" before opening the door.

"It's me, Hudson," came the reply.

I opened the door. One look at his face and I knew he didn't have good news for me. "What's wrong?" I asked.

"I just noticed that the padlock on your locker is hanging open. Any chance you forgot to snick it shut?"

"Not another break-in!"

"I'm so sorry," Hudson said. "We've never had problems like this before." I wondered if he was implying that somehow I was to blame for ruining the marina's unblemished record. Well, maybe I was.

Even though it seemed unnecessary, given that someone had already searched my office, I shut and locked my office door before going to check out my locker. Hudson came with me.

"Does it look like someone tampered with the locks on any of the other lockers?" I asked. Hudson assured me that only my locker was involved. Lucky me.

The lockers are lined up in a recess under the parking area. They've been there forever, their wood doors weathered by time. No one expected them to be very secure, and I couldn't imagine that anyone kept anything valuable in any of them. That said, I've always assumed that no one would bother breaking in.

When I removed the unlocked padlock and looked inside my locker, I felt like someone had punched me in the stomach. It was as if a tornado had touched down inside. Everything was topsy-turvy. Boxes upended. Papers scattered everywhere.

Smatterings of glass. Pottery I'd made in a class years ago turned into shards. Boat fenders slashed. All in all, an incredible mess.

"Oh my god," Hudson said as he peered over my shoulder.

I was too stunned to say anything. Which was probably a good thing. Because I might have uttered some very unladylike oaths. What I couldn't imagine was how they had done so much damage without being heard or seen by someone. By the time I'd internalized what I was looking at I was able to censor and moderate my response. "Pretty bad, huh?"

"Terrible," Hudson said with feeling. "Who would do something like this?"

"Someone who hates goldfish," I said.

"Huh?"

"I think it was the same person who killed Bubbles III."

"Is someone mad at you?" Hudson asked.

I actually laughed. "That's the understatement of the year."

a low profile

I t seemed like everyone was irritated with me. The "Say No to Chimeras" people had expelled me from their group. Jared's parents were hot and bothered about the "thing" I had taken from their son. My mother was annoyed because she couldn't understand why I was so hard on such a "nice young man" as Keith. The police were upset because they were convinced there was something I wasn't telling them. Judd was undoubtedly tired of the *Aspara* being tied up next to the *Carpe Diem*. And whoever was breaking into my personal spaces was obviously pissed because they weren't finding what they were looking for.

Before leaving my office, I'd tried to find pictures of Jared Blaine's parents on social media without success. I'd been hoping for Facebook photos, but that would have been too easy. Even Macavity was peeved with me. I still hadn't purchased any of his favorite snacks, and he seemed to resent having to walk across the *Carpe Diem* to get home. He's never liked change.

At least Logan and Sophie were on my side, although they were both slightly miffed that I wasn't taking their advice to get out of town until everything calmed down. Ben, of course, wanted me on the first stagecoach out of town too.

I was fixing myself a toasted cheese sandwich for dinner when

Bill called. He wanted to let me know that he had been approached by a rival of NorPac to discuss a possible job with them. He was fairly certain they thought he knew more about Jared's research than he did. Otherwise he couldn't imagine why they would offer him a position at almost twice what he was currently getting paid.

"I'm going to meet with them tomorrow," he said. "Any suggestions?"

"*Oh no,*" I shouted.

"What?!" he said.

"Oh, nooo," I repeated, half shout and half groan as Macavity howled in alarm.

My toasted cheese sandwich was burning. A thick puff of smoke spiraled upward and fanned out across the tongue and groove wood ceiling.

I pulled the fry pan off the stove and looked around for some place to set it down.

"What's happening?" Bill asked loudly.

"Just a minute," I said more calmly than I felt.

Finally locating a trivet, I put the pan on it and flipped the burned sandwich onto a plate. The acrid smell of burned bread filled the tiny cabin. Macavity jumped up on the table to sniff at the sandwich and quickly backed off, glaring at me for ruining something he would have been willing to share. He loves cheese.

"Sorry," I said to Bill. "I had something on the stove."

"Do you want to call me back?"

"No, it's fine now." Well, not really. I was low on supplies and had just ruined my best chance at a comfort meal. Trying to regain my focus, I said, "So you're wondering how to find out whether they want to hire you because of what you know about Jared's project."

"Yes."

"Won't they ask you what you've been working on?"

"Well, yes."

"And won't that give you an opportunity to distinguish your-self from Jared?"

"But what if that's the reason they want me to come to work for them?"

"Once it's established that you don't have the information they want, do you think they will back out of the offer? Is that your concern?"

"I don't think you get it, Bryn."

"What don't I get?"

"First of all, it would be a big step up for me. But second, they could be behind what happened to Jared."

"So, if they *think* you know more than you do and you take the job and then they find out you don't know what they thought you did . . ."

"There goes the job."

"And if they're responsible for Jared's death, you definitely don't want to go to work for them, no matter what the salary is."

"What do I do?"

I didn't have to give it much thought. "I don't think you have a choice. You need to go to the interview and assess the situation."

"But what if they offer me the job?"

"Then you say you need to think about it. You don't have to make a decision on the spot."

Bill sighed. "I've been with NorPac and HHC since I got out of school, so I'm not very good at this."

"Let me see what I can find out about them, okay?"

"Would you? That would be great." He gave me the name of the company and his contact there. I promised to get on it first thing in the morning.

"One last thing," I said. "Any chance you ever met Jared's parents?"

"Yes, one time. Why?"

"Could you describe them?"

"Why?"

"It's complicated—could you just describe them for me?"

Bill thought a long time before responding. It was a good thing he wasn't being called as an eyewitness in a criminal case. Still, the way he depicted the couple was close enough. They were probably the real thing. But that didn't explain why they thought I had something that belonged to their son and why they had reacted so mysteriously.

As soon as I hung up, I opened the hatch to dissipate the smell. Seconds later I heard Logan yell, "Is something burning?"

"Yes, it *was*," I yelled back.

Logan stepped aboard the *Aspara* and peered at me through the open hatch. "I hope that wasn't dinner."

"That's the operative word—*was*."

"We're just about to have spaghetti with my special sauce." Logan was always coming up with a new "special" sauce to try and capture the way his grandmother used to make spaghetti. Each time he was convinced that *this* would be it, but I was convinced it was one of those childhood memories that cannot be relived.

"I can't keep bumming meals off you," I said, hoping he'd persuade me otherwise.

"Sure you can. Come on."

That was all it took. I eagerly climbed up the companionway and followed Logan across to the *Carpe Diem*. Macavity howled again, this time from the aft deck of the *Aspara*. I turned back and said, "Sorry, Judd won't want you to join us. I promise I'll go shopping tomorrow." As if he understood but didn't approve, Macavity sped across the *Carpe Diem* and leapt onto the dock. "He seems a bit testy of late," Logan commented.

"He thinks the universe revolves around him."

"Don't we all."

After a delicious dinner that, from Logan's perspective, still didn't quite live up to his dreams of the past, I told Judd and Logan about the offer the NorPac rival, MedTech, had made Bill. They both knew of the company. Judd's firm had done some legal work for them a few years back. He told me that their corporate headquarters was in Chicago, but they had a large footprint in the area as well as an international presence in the medical technology world. Logan had followed their rise in the stock market and had considered investing some money in their stock.

"So, are they an ethical company?" I asked.

"What can I say?" Judd commented. "I only handled some of the ancillary paperwork. But as far as I know, they didn't quibble about costs and paid their bills on time."

"Any large organization can employ underhanded or aggressive tactics to get what they want," Logan added.

"And," Judd said, "in the race to be first to acquire new products, there's a lot of money at stake. Bill needs to watch his back."

"If I were him," Logan said, "I'd make sure they knew I had absolutely nothing to do with Blaine's research. If they still make him an offer, then he'll know it's based on his own merit."

"Hey," Judd said suddenly, "what's that noise?" We all stopped talking and listened.

"Frogs," I said. "My phone." I jumped up and made a beeline for the *Aspara*, yelling, "Thanks for dinner," over my shoulder.

It was Fiona. I made it just in time to answer before she was switched over to voice mail. We chatted for some time, exchanging information and speculating about what was going on and what I should do next. In answer to the question I'd left for her earlier, she confirmed what I'd already suspected, the Scottish police claimed not to have talked to the Blaines nor given them any information about me or the backpack. Nor had her rescue team colleagues. And, although Fiona understood why I didn't want to completely back off, she cautioned that I needed to keep a low profile.

"We don't know who is pulling the strings on this," she said. "But they are obviously determined to get whatever it is they are looking for. And they seem to think you may have the key. So, you need to be careful, very careful."

Logan appeared just after I got off the phone. "Not much privacy, tied up side by side like this," he said.

"How much did you hear?"

"Bits and pieces of your side of the conversation. So . . .?"

I filled him in while making two cups of tea. Logan made a face when he took the first sip of his. "What *is* this?" he asked.

"Mango. Isn't it good?" Logan and I both prefer black teas to anything herbal or fruity, but for some reason I love this tea. I buy it online from a small shop in Hawaii.

Logan sniffed it. "It does smell good. But . . ."

"Try it. You may end up liking it."

He took a tentative sip and smacked his lips. I smiled.

"What's so funny?" he asked.

"You. You remind me of Macavity in many ways."

On cue, Macavity leapt down the steps and jumped up into Logan's lap. It made me smile even more. Macavity's fur has a slightly more orange tint than Logan's hair, but they aren't many shades off. My hair is a darker red, and I only have a smattering of freckles. Whereas Logan probably looked like a version of Tom Sawyer when he was young. He hates his freckles, but I find them appealingly boyish.

"I'll take that as a compliment," Logan said as he stroked Macavity's belly.

"So, what do you think? Really? If I take Ben's advice and go away for a week and nothing is resolved, what do I do then?" We agreed that going away was only a temporary solution. But we also agreed there were certain lines of inquiry that were more dangerous than others. Like trying to find out if Jared's parents were acting on their own. Or continuing to poke around in the affairs of the "Say No to Chimeras" group. Even trying to learn more about Keith's agenda seemed problematic. We did, however, decide it might be interesting to investigate whether there were any groups in Scotland opposed to the type of research Blaine had been doing and, if so, whether all of these protest groups were networked. It seemed entirely possible we could check out the various groups online without calling attention to ourselves.

After much discussion, our plan for Tuesday included me

calling Ben about Jared's parents, Logan setting up a meeting with a friend of his from the school of business at the University to see what he knew about MedTech, and following through with Bill. And, if there was any time left over, we would see what we could find out about anti-chimera groups in Europe. Perhaps not an entirely low-profile approach, but hopefully not one that would put one or both of us in the crosshairs of the bad guys.

It had been a long day. After Logan left, Macavity and I called it a night.

big bad wolf

For the first time since getting back from Scotland I woke up on my own just before the alarm went off. Of course, it might have had something to do with the fact that Macavity was sitting on my chest again, nuzzling my chin with the top of his head. I like to think it's an expression of affection rather than simply an attempt to wake me up to get him his breakfast.

I rubbed him behind the ears the way he likes and said, "Good morning, Macavity. How's my favorite cat this morning?" I always think it's a bit weird when people talk to their pets—unless they are giving a command—but I do it anyway. And it wouldn't surprise me if some day Macavity says something back. Needless to say, he would most likely clam up after that and make me doubt whether I'd actually heard him speak.

While enjoying my morning coffee I called Ben and filled him in on the visit from Jared's parents and the information Fiona had passed along. He was as surprised by the visit as I had been.

"What puzzles me most is how they found out about the backpack, if not from the police. Or from the rescue team."

"What about his colleague at NorPac, could he have told them?"

"He knows I didn't get anything from the pack, so what motivation could he have had to make that up?"

"Is there anyone else you told about the pack?"

"You."

"I think you can cross me off the list."

"I already did."

"And you're absolutely certain the Scottish police didn't tell them anything."

"Fiona checked. Besides, they still think Blaine's off hiking somewhere."

Ben was silent a moment. Then he said, "There's something here that doesn't make sense."

"I know what you mean. If they believe their son is alive, then why come to see me? And if they know he's dead—"

"Okay, let's walk through this. We know that his laptop and tablet are missing, right?"

"Right."

"And it's possible someone other than the killer thinks you have them."

"Someone *might* think that, if they assume I removed them from his backpack. But doesn't it seem unlikely he had them with him while hiking in the rain? And why was he even there on that trail in the first place? That still bothers me."

"Maybe someone is assuming that because you were staying at the same place and were both from Seattle that there was more of a connection than there was. Is that possible?"

"I suppose it's possible." Ben's reference to us staying at the same inn was an opening to tell him that I had searched Blaine's room, but I held back. I didn't see what relevance it had, and I was certain he wouldn't approve. Besides, no one knew I had done that, except for Logan and Sophie.

Ben sighed. "I don't know what to say. But what I *do* know is that we need to make sure the Blaines understand that you don't have anything that belongs to their son. I'll talk with them."

"Don't be too hard on them," I said. "After all, at some

point they are going to find out that their son is dead. Although why they aren't more concerned with his whereabouts and less with whatever it is they think I took, I don't understand."

I had barely finished my second cup of coffee when Logan appeared. We were going to meet his friend at the University at 10:30 for coffee. More coffee. Oh well. That gave me just enough time to run to the store and pick up a few things before getting swallowed up by the tasks before us.

At 10:30 Logan and I were in a coffee shop in the basement of an old building on campus. The wood walls with their ornate cornices looked like they could have been there since the reign of Queen Victoria. There were also several hefty wood beams overhead that could probably support a herd of elephants carousing on the floor above. Even the wood tables and chairs and the stone fireplace looked like something left over from a European turn-of-the-century movie set. The place definitely had atmosphere. And the coffee was good.

When Logan told me the name of his friend was Gray Alexander, I immediately pictured a tall, handsome man with elegant bearing and fashionable clothes. A swashbuckling demeanor and smoke-colored eyes. The truth was disappointing. As he approached our table, I guessed he was about three inches shorter than me, all elbows and whacked out hair, and he was wearing a cardigan. Hadn't anyone told him they had gone out of fashion in the 70s? Maybe before that even.

Up close he was somewhat more impressive. His handshake was firm, his dark eyes lively, and he had a voice to rival Morgan Freeman's. I instantly liked him and found myself wondering whether he was married. Oh, oh, I was thinking like Sophie. Cultural conditioning can be hard to overcome.

Logan gave Gray the background we had agreed to share with him, and Gray immediately launched into a professorial lecture on corporate spying and dirty tricks. After about five minutes, I interrupted and asked, "But what do you know specifically about

MedTech, anything?" Fortunately, he didn't seem offended by my rude "get-to-the-point" interruption.

"If you're asking whether I know for a fact that they engage in any illegal or unethical activities, no, I don't. On the other hand, they are in a highly competitive industry where getting to the market first with a new product can be critical."

"Do you know whether they are interested in the biotech research NorPac is into?"

"What biotechnology company wouldn't be? The fact that they are known for their work on genetically altered plants, plant materials. and food products doesn't mean they aren't interested in other lines of research. Especially in an area where there's big money at stake. As you may know, there's a critical shortage of human organs nationally and internationally. The current illegal market trading in human organs is huge. The potential for turning a gigantic profit with breakthrough technology is tremendous."

"I get the idea that you think any greedy corporate execs might be tempted to go to extremes to get their hands on this kind of information."

"Absolutely. And most scientists are aware of who is doing what and how close they are to finding answers. This research takes years and years to complete, and scientists, for the most part, tend to share what they are learning. There's also the urge to boast about successes."

"And I would imagine there are *some scientists* who wouldn't be averse to making a fortune."

"I don't think you can assume that all scientists are devoting themselves to their research for the good of humanity. Science is science, but the love of money tends to be universal."

"You don't' know anyone at MedTech that we could talk to, do you?" Logan asked. We had agreed we wouldn't pursue any leads publicly, but I admit that I was wondering the same thing.

"Corporate espionage is by its very nature covert. I doubt any average employee could or would tell you much." He paused and looked from Logan to me and back again. "I take it there is something serious involved here."

Logan and I glanced at each other, trying to decide how much more to tell Gray. Finally, I said, "I didn't ask to get mixed up in any kind of corporate espionage, but for some reason there is someone out there who thinks I have information about some cutting-edge stem cell research that I don't have. And they are getting pretty aggressive in trying to make me give it up. We believe that someone at MedTech might be behind it all."

"Have you gone to the police?" Gray frowned. "Sorry, stupid question. I assume you don't have any real proof or you wouldn't be sitting here asking me for a contact." He tugged at his left ear and seemed to be considering something. "Okay," he said after a few seconds of silence, "I know someone who might know something about whether MedTech is interested in what NorPac is working on. I'll talk to him."

"We can't ask you to do that," Logan said.

Gray smiled. "Too dangerous?"

"As you said, if they are determined to acquire something, these people don't consider themselves bound by the same rules the rest of us adhere to." I paused. "And there's already been one death."

Gray stared at me. "And you think someone from MedTech may be responsible?"

"I don't know," I admitted. "But it's a possibility."

Logan and I sat there watching Gray process the information. It didn't take him long to decide. "Well, that means I will need to be careful, doesn't it?"

Our next stop was to meet Bill for lunch. On the way Logan and I talked about whether we had been wise to approach Gray.

"He could end up getting us all in trouble," I said. "All it takes is one little slip-up."

"He's a smart man," Logan said. "He knows what he's up against."

"We could call him off."

"For some reason I don't think that would prevent him from talking to his contact at this point, do you?"

"No, I think we've piqued his curiosity. But if he's going to talk to someone at MedTech, I hope his contact will be discreet."

"Maybe it's the wife of the CEO," Logan said with a sly smile.

"What?"

"Did I mention he's quite the womanizer?"

"No, and Gray doesn't give off that kind of vibe."

"Weren't you attracted to him?" Logan looked at me with a "gotcha" grin.

"You didn't warn me," I said.

"A fling might be a good thing for you."

I didn't bother responding because we'd arrived at our destination. But he was right, I could use a good fling.

Lunch with Bill was painful. In spite of our earlier conversation, he had apparently let himself believe that the job offer from MedTech was sincere. But during the interview he had done what I advised and made it clear that he had not been involved in Jared's research and didn't currently have access to any of the project data. He said that as soon as that came out, their interest in him visibly waned. The interview ended shortly after that with the promise that they would be in touch. It was no consolation that he already had a good job that he liked. He had allowed himself to dream, and the dream had been crushed.

Afterward, Logan and I agreed that if MedTech was in essence the big bad wolf hoping to use their cunning to get what they wanted, their disguise wasn't very good. They were looking more and more like any other company on the make. A company that was possibly willing to try subterfuge and threats to get what they wanted. But murder? And, if they had approached the Blaines, what could they have offered to get them involved?

We felt we were onto something, but we weren't quite sure what that something was.

———

That evening both Logan and I went online to read about chimera research and protests in Europe and around the world. Although the US and Western Europe were regulated by strict codes of ethics, there seemed to be a lot of variation in regulatory framework. And there was nothing to suggest that other countries such as China were in alignment with the US and Western Europe on where to draw the line. Or even on agreeing that there *was* a line.

Two big ethical and legal questions kept popping up. Did the creation of human-chimera diminish the dignity of being human? And, should chimera be granted legal rights? These issues were on the table for discussion in some countries, but it wasn't clear if they were even on the radar for others.

During the last couple of years there had been quite a few protests in Western Europe over genetic modifications to humans, stem cell research and creating chimeras. But there didn't seem to be a centralized movement, just groups here and there trying to gain the attention of a busy and indifferent citizenry.

In the original version of Little Red Riding Hood, the wolf swallows the girl. But in the Grimm's' version, there is a happy ending. She learns her lesson and becomes wise. If the big bad wolf was biotech research, I could only hope that the public learned their lesson before we were all swallowed up.

you have 24 hours

Wednesday morning Macavity and I had a serious talk about whether we should continue rafting to the *Carpe Diem*. Both of us wanted to go back to our home base. But deep down I wasn't sure it was a good idea.

"I'm sorry," I concluded. "I understand how you feel. But we're going to be stuck here a little longer."

"Murf," Macavity said as he woofed down his breakfast.

"Bryn? You there?" Logan called.

"Come on down."

As Logan scooched around to the back of the settee he said,

"I heard you talking to someone." It was half question.

"Just Macavity."

"Oh."

"Don't say it . . .," I warned.

Logan laughed. "Don't worry, you know I sometimes talk to myself."

"It's not the same," I argued.

"Oh?" Logan gave me the stink eye. "Was Macavity one of Jared's experiments?"

We both looked at Macavity. I tried to imagine what he would be like with a few human cells in his brain. "Terrifying thought," I said.

"Maybe Bubbles and Macavity could go to grad school together."

"Thinking about how different one of your classes might look?"

"Like a Star Wars bar scene."

"Bryn to Logan," I intoned. "Return to earth."

"Okay. Just wanted to check in before I head for the U. You going to be alright today?"

"Low profile, remember?"

"Well, if you need anything, give me a shout." He reached over, swiped my coffee cup, and drained it. "Good coffee," he said as he climbed up the steps. Macavity followed him.

I straightened up the main cabinet and headed for my office. When I arrived, I was surprised to see someone waiting for me.

It was Conrad, Sophie's friend from the "Say No to Chimeras" group. And he didn't look happy.

"Hi, Conrad," I said.

"Hi, Bryn. Got a minute?"

"Sure." I unlocked the two locks to my office and stepped inside, holding the door open for him. He walked directly over to the chair in front of my desk and sat down. I shut the door and took a seat behind my desk across from him. "What can I do for you?" I asked.

Conrad took a deep breath and then laid it all out for me. His fellow members were unhappy with him for inviting me to a meeting. And he felt like I had used him. Furthermore, not only did they think I was spying on them, but they were also convinced I was somehow in cahoots with Jared Blaine. Conrad admitted that some of the group members had been applying "pressure" on Blaine to end his research and that they thought he had gone into hiding to finish his project. Furthermore, they believed that I knew where he was.

"And you want me to tell you where to find him?"

"Sophie says you are a reasonable person. She claims you wanted to attend a few meetings to get a sense of what the group was all about. Not to gather information for Blaine or the police or to sabotage our work."

"Sophie's right," I said. "And I don't know where Blaine is. I've never even met him." Unless you counted seeing his corpse as an introduction.

Conrad did a retake. "Then what were the two of you doing in Scotland together?"

"We weren't together. I just happened to be staying at the same inn as he was when he went missing. I took an interest because he was from Seattle."

"That doesn't quite make sense."

There was no way I was going to tell Conrad about finding Blaine's body. Improvising a little, I said, "But I do know someone who works with him. And he's concerned about what's happened to his friend. He should have been back before now. Or called or texted or something."

"So, was that why you wanted to attend one of our meetings, to find out if we knew what had happened to him?"

"That was part of it."

"Then you *do* think something has happened to him." I could tell Conrad was starting to put the pieces of the puzzle together. "But you don't think someone in our group is responsible for his disappearance, do you?"

"It has crossed my mind."

"That's a serious accusation," Conrad said.

"Maybe they wanted his data, and something went wrong," I suggested. "Or maybe they wanted to *destroy* his data, and something went wrong."

"But—" Conrad apparently couldn't think of a comeback. He probably knew better than anyone what a few extremists were capable of.

"We know that his laptop is missing, and so is he. What do *you* think has happened?"

"His laptop is missing?" Conrad sounded sincerely surprised.

"And I don't have it, or anything associated with him or with his research. Nothing. Nada." I held up my hands for emphasis. "And if I'd come across his laptop, I would have given it to NorPac. Like it or not, they own the data. But I never met the man and I don't have anything belonging to him."

"You do understand how dangerous Blaine's research could be in the wrong hands?"

"I'm not sure how I feel about his research," I said truthfully. "But I've given quite a bit of thought as to what could go wrong. And I think I understand at least some of the ethical and legal issues involved. I'm actually sympathetic with your cause. But I don't see how I can help you."

Conrad leaned back in the chair. He seemed deflated. "If you're telling the truth . . ."

"I am," I assured him.

"Then we've got a problem."

"We?"

"There are a couple of people who are convinced you either know where he is or are in possession of his research data. I came here today because of my regard for Sophie. I wanted to persuade you to give him, or it, up to keep you out of harm's way."

"So, you think these people you're referring to are dangerous?"

Conrad looked reluctant to admit that someone in his group could be a threat to my well-being, but otherwise, why would he be sitting across from me?

"Are these the same people who took a shot at me at the demonstration?" I asked.

"Someone shot at you?" Conrad looked sincerely surprised for the second time.

"I was lucky the bullet only grazed my arm," I said. "But it would have been worse if a friend hadn't pulled me out of harm's way."

"I didn't know." Conrad looked truly shaken.

"What about my goldfish?" I asked, pressing my case.

His eyes went to Bubbles IV swimming around and around in his tiny water world. "That goldfish?" he asked.

"A previous fish. I've replaced him," I said. "But someone put this letter opener . . ." I picked up the dagger that Ben had returned to me and held it in front of Conrad. "Someone stabbed my last goldfish with this and left him pinned to my desk." I shoved the files aside and pointed to the place where the point had gone in.

He looked at the gash in my desk and back at Bubbles IV.

"That doesn't sound like something anyone in the group would do."

"What about shooting at me? Does that sound like something they would do?"

Conrad looked down. Then he shook his head. "I don't know."

"What about trying to break into my boat? And searching my office? And tossing my locker?"

"That's happened?" he asked. I nodded. Conrad sighed and said, "To be honest, that all seems possible." I was tempted to say something about the illegality of invading other people's property, but I didn't feel like I was on solid ethical ground given some of the things I'd done in the past.

"So, where are we?" I asked.

Conrad looked crestfallen. Like he had just learned that Pluto was no longer considered a planet. "I don't know," he repeated.

I felt a little sorry for him. And somewhat responsible for his predicament. "How about a cup of coffee?"

He accepted my offer of coffee and agreed to talk about what he and I should or could do to defuse the situation. Brainstorming possible courses of action to reach a goal was something I did all the time with clients, so I got out a flipchart pad and set it up on a stand. Conrad seemed a bit taken aback by the formality of the process I was proposing, but he agreed to participate. Unfortunately, after listing all the facts we knew and all of the possible actions we could take to prevent things from escalating, we weren't much further along than we'd been at the start of the exercise.

"Bottom line is that you don't think they will believe that I'm not in any way connected with Blaine. But *you* believe me?" He nodded.

"Why?

"Because I know Sophie. Besides, you don't seem like the type."

People seemed to be assessing what my *type* was a lot lately. In this instance, I wasn't sure exactly what he meant, but I decided it was probably better under the circumstances to not be that type.

"And you can't think of any way I can convince them of my innocence?"

"Not the two people I mentioned. And they are very influential within the group. Because of their passion for the cause. And . . . because they are kinda scary."

"Great. That makes me feel so good."

We both stared at the lists we had compiled, as if expecting to suddenly see a solution. But nothing leapt out at us. There were no revelations, no aha moments. Just words on a chart. I could apparently help clients find answers to their problems using this approach, but when it really counted, when it was a possible life and death situation for me, the process fell short.

"I know you don't want to tell me their names," I said, looking at him for confirmation. "And I assume you wouldn't be willing to make an anonymous call to the police." He shook his head. "And I also assume you want to help me stay alive."

"Stay alive?" he echoed as if he hadn't realized how high the stakes might be.

"How do you think they are going to try to get the information out of me if they can't find it among my possessions? And you said yourself that they probably won't believe that I don't know anything."

"I can't imagine . . ."

"They shot me," I interrupted, my voice louder than I'd intended. "A few inches to my right and I wouldn't be here for this nice little chat with you."

"You can't go to the police," he said.

"Actually, I can. Unless you can come up with something better."

He stood up. "I need to talk to some of the other group members. See what they think." He started for the door.

"You have twenty-four hours," I said, feeling a little like a Liam Neeson movie character.

He turned back toward me. "Just don't go to the police yet, okay?"

I nodded, not really sure I meant it. But this was one lie I could tell with a clear conscience.

I worked out of my office the rest of the morning. There was plenty to do, but I had difficulty focusing. Every so often I would find myself watching Bubbles IV, staring at him as he swam around and around. It was comforting. For me at least; perhaps not for him.

At lunch time I took a break and walked over to the cafe to buy a sandwich. I brought it back and ate it at the tiny table on my deck, hoping the sun would come out from behind the dark sky overhead. But the sky remained cloudy, like my thoughts about what to do next. Unless Conrad managed to talk some sense into the "Say No" people, I wasn't sure what I should do.

After consuming the last of my sandwich, I found myself pacing around and around my desk while trying to make a decision, a human version of Bubbles IV.

By late afternoon I was feeling totally out of control. So, when Logan stopped by on his way home, I greeted him like a long-lost friend. Sensing my need to talk, he came in and sat down. I immediately told him about Conrad dropping by and showed him the lists we'd made, including what I'd added based on information I hadn't shared with Conrad.

"It's like starting in the middle of a novel," Logan said. "A novel with no closing chapters."

"It feels like we should be able to extrapolate in both directions. What led to the items on these lists, and what the most reasonable next steps are."

"You sound like a college professor."

"And your point is?"

"Too bad you aren't a detective."

"That *is* what you need," he said.

"Oh no, I'm not calling Ben."

"You don't have to give Conrad twenty-four hours."

"But if I don't give him a chance to get back to me, what reason do we have to believe he will give up the names to Ben?"

"What if we have Sophie talk to him?"

"I'm having dinner with her tonight. I'll see what she thinks."

Logan ran his hands over key points on the chart as if he could make them come to life by touching them. "Okay," he concluded. "*I'll* give *you* twenty hours."

<hr>

When I went back to the *Aspara* to change for dinner, Logan came out as I crossed the *Carpe Diem* to ask me whether I felt I should go alone to meet Sophie. I started to dismiss his concerns, then hesitated. "Want to join us?" I asked. It would be nice to have someone with me when I drove home in the dark.

"You buying?"

"I think the bodyguard stays outside and waits in the car."

"Not *this* bodyguard."

"Then, yes, I'll buy."

Sophie and Logan are not best friends, but they are comfortable with each other. And she immediately guessed why he was with me. "Good idea," she whispered to me as we joined her, without specifically referring to what the good idea was. That's why it's nice to have friends you have known for a long time. You don't have as much explaining to do.

We had a pleasant dinner, chatting about inconsequential things, relaxing. When we reached our after-dinner coffee, I brought up Conrad's visit and told her about our conversation. "What do you think?" I asked in conclusion. "Should I trust Conrad to follow through?"

"And do you think he can do so safely?" Logan interjected.

Selfishly, I hadn't thought about Conrad's safety, just my own. Another reason not to involve Sophie more.

"They obviously don't know Blaine is dead," Sophie said.

"At least they are acting as if they don't."

"I'm not so sure about that," Logan said to me. "Maybe the two guys Conrad is referring to know Jared is dead and one or both were in the woods when you picked up the backpack."

As if on cue, each of us took a sip of coffee, contemplating the possibility.

"You can't wait," Sophie concluded. "You need to tell Ben about this."

"I'm not so sure. I feel like I need to give Conrad a chance to see what he can find out."

"I vote for telling Ben," Logan said. I was beginning to be sorry I'd invited him along. Although I had to ask myself why I asked for advice if I wasn't going to take it.

"I'd talk with Conrad if I thought it would do any good," Sophie offered. "But he's either going to tell you or he isn't. And either way, this is something for the police to handle."

Logan nodded agreement.

"If Ben approaches him, I think he will deny everything. Let's give him just a little more time, okay? If I don't hear from him by noon tomorrow, I'll call Ben." I looked from Sophie to Logan and back to Sophie. After a few moments of silence, they reluctantly agreed. If the information didn't come by tomorrow at high noon, I would resort to Plan B.

When we left the restaurant, we stood in the doorway a few minutes, checking to see if there was anyone hanging around outside or if there were any suspicious looking people sitting in nearby cars. It felt strange to think that kind of caution was necessary, and I had my doubts about whether we would be able to accurately assess the situation anyway. Still, as far as we could tell, everything looked normal.

On the way back to the marina, we stayed on side streets, constantly checking out the other cars we saw. We even tried a couple of maneuvers to see if anyone stayed with us. It felt surreal, like we were playing a game, us against them. But my arm was still sore where the bullet had grazed me. That proved it was real.

No one followed us from the restaurant, no one we saw at least. And there was no one waiting in the shadows for us at the marina. Again, no one that we saw, and no one that leapt out at us.

I was relieved to get safely back to my sailboat home and call it a night. But I had a hard time falling asleep. I tossed and turned in time with my fluctuating thoughts. What had happened to Blaine's laptop and tablet? It seemed like everyone was looking for one or both. Even the people most likely to have killed him. All I knew for sure was that I didn't have either of them; I'd never even seen them.

So why did everyone assume that they were in my possession? Hopefully I would have a lead by high noon.

CHAPTER 21

a lie of omission

The morning started off with my usual routines. Make and drink coffee. Feed Macavity. Choose which pair of jeans to wear. Decide which shirt didn't need laundering. Walk to my office. Consider and reject the possibility of cleaning up the clutter. Feed Bubbles IV. Review my "to do" list. Pick something from the list. And officially start the day.

I was making good progress on structuring a retreat I was going to do for a client when there was an urgent knock on the door, a harsh, quick rapping that demanded immediate attention.

"Who is it?" I asked through the door. I had a bad vibe about what was going to happen next.

"Marie and John Blaine" a female voice impatiently responded. The tone said, "Open up!" I did.

"We need to talk." Marie Blaine almost knocked me over as she pushed past me and took the chair in front of my desk. John looked apologetic as he retrieved the fold-up chair he had used before. Apologetic but determined.

I sat down behind my desk. "Did Detective Peterson get in touch with you?" I thought he was going to handle the Blaines and that I wouldn't need to see them again. Unless . . .

"Yes," Mrs. Blaine said. "He came to see us Tuesday afternoon."

She was either really quick on the uptake, or they'd met with Ben. Which suggested they were probably the real thing. "I thought he would clear up any misunderstandings you might have about my, ah, role in your son's, ah, disappearance." It was hard to keep on deceiving them about their son. But I didn't feel I had a choice.

"There was something we didn't tell Detective Peterson," Mrs. Blaine began, glancing at her husband. He gave her a go-ahead nod.

She took out a Kleenex and dabbed at her eyes before continuing. "Someone is holding Jared hostage," she said, her voice shaking with emotion. Her husband reached out and put a hand on her shoulder. She grasped his hand and squeezed. "You finish telling her, John. I . . . I can't."

"You see," he said. "They told us not to go to the police. They said if we could convince you to give up whatever it was you took from his pack, they would release him."

"Did they say what they thought I took?"

Mr. Blaine took a deep breath. "They said it could have been a laptop or a tablet or both. Maybe even a thumb drive."

"So, why didn't you just ask me if I had any of those? Why be so mysterious?"

"We thought it was best if you thought we knew specifically what you had taken."

"But you understand, don't you, that I didn't take anything? That I don't have any of those items?"

Mrs. Blaine jumped in, sounding stronger, and desperate.

"But why would they think that you did if you aren't involved?"

"I'm not sure. Maybe because I showed some interest in his research. Maybe because I was in Scotland staying at the same inn with your son. But I can assure you, they are way off base."

She continued to glare at me. Her husband, on the other

hand, looked from his wife to me and back to her again, as if waiting for someone to give him his next lines. Finally, he said, "Look, this isn't the first time Jared has been a target because of what he does. Or the first time he's had problems because of it. I mean, we're proud of him and his accomplishments, but we understand why some people don't want him to succeed."

"These people who claim to have your son, I assume you didn't meet them face to face."

"No, it was all handled over the phone."

"Any proof that they are actually holding him hostage?" That would be tricky, I thought.

"No," Mrs. Blaine said, "but he's definitely not answering his phone or email or . . ." Her voice gave out and she took out the Kleenex again.

"Can you tell me a little about the problems you mentioned that he's had in the past?"

"Well," Mr. Blaine said, looking to his wife for approval. "You probably know about the 'Say No to Chimeras' protests. And the fire at NorPac. But there have been other things. He's always getting nasty tweets and threatening emails. One guy accused him of being a tool of the devil. Followed him everywhere carrying a sign with Jared's face with devil horns sticking out of his head. Jared had to get a restraining order on him."

"And don't forget about the couple who wanted a kidney for their daughter," Mrs. Blaine said.

"Oh, yeah. Her parents wanted Jared to use her as part of an experiment. Grow a kidney for her. Of course, he had to refuse, and they were very upset."

"I would think that a young girl would be high on a transplant list."

"She had other health issues, so she wasn't a good candidate under any circumstances. But that didn't make her parents any less insistent."

"Surely they didn't have a doctor who was willing to perform the operation, even if Jared had agreed and been able to produce a compatible kidney."

"The parents weren't being rational. Especially the mother. I think she had a breakdown when her daughter died."

"And," Mrs. Blaine interjected, "Jared isn't at his best when dealing with emotional people. He's a scientist. Not a people person."

"Did you speak to these parents?"

"We were there one time when they came by to plead with Jared to give their daughter a chance. It was heartbreaking. I mean, Jared was right—he couldn't do what they were asking. But, well, he could have been more sympathetic. He basically told them they had to accept that their daughter was going to die and move on with their lives."

Mr. Blaine added, "They also went after the girl's doctor. They were mad at him for not trying harder to get her a kidney. You may have read about the incident at the hospital where they were screaming and threatening to sue him and had to be hauled away by the police."

I didn't remember reading about it, but I could picture the story. *Distraught parents accuse doctor of being unwilling to help their dying daughter.* People faced with the imminent death of a loved one always hoped for a miracle. But what these parents had been asking for seemed to me to require a whole series of miracles. I felt sorry for everyone involved.

"And the people who contacted you about Jared, any hint of who they might be or what they want the information for?"

Mrs. Blaine jumped in, out of control again. "What difference does it make who they are or what they want to do with the information? We need to give them what they want. We need to get our son back."

I took a deep breath. "I want you to know that if there was any way I could help, I would. But I don't have his laptop or his tablet or any other device containing his research information. I wish I did, but I don't. I'm sorry. Very sorry."

Mrs. Blaine leaned forward and put her face in her hands. "What are we going to do?" she asked no one in particular.

Mr. Blaine patted her back. "We'll figure something out," he said, not sounding at all like he believed what he was saying.

"I know they told you not to go to the police, but you need to tell Detective Peterson what you've told me."

"We can't," Mrs. Blaine said as she sat up and dried her eyes. "They said we would never see our son again if we did."

A wave of guilt threatened to engulf me. I wanted to blurt out the truth. End the pain of uncertainty. The pain to come would be worse in many ways, but at least they would be able to get on with their grieving instead of remaining in limbo. It was all so complicated. There was no body, no support for my claims. If I told them what I knew, the Blaines would end up with another version of painful uncertainty.

"And *you* can't tell him," Mr. Blaine said. "If you do . . ." He didn't seem entirely certain as to what he was threatening to do if I told Detective Peterson about their visit, but he sounded resolute.

I believe that being transparent and honest with people is usually the best course of action. But in this instance, all of my instincts were to lie. There was no way I could tell them the truth about their son. And I would definitely have to tell Ben about their visit.

"I'm so sorry I can't help you," was all I said. That at least was the truth.

After they left, I called Ben, but he didn't answer. I left a message for him to call me as soon as he could. Then I turned back to my work on the retreat, but I couldn't concentrate. The next thing I knew I was trying to find the name of the girl Jared had refused to experiment on. The Blaines had asked if I'd read about the incident between her doctor and her parents, so that's where I started, searching for newspaper coverage. It didn't take long to find something.

Both local TV stations and the local newspaper had briefly

covered the poignant human-interest story. One article referred to the "grief-stricken parents" and their "tragic situation." It showed a picture of them with their young son standing next to their daughter's hospital bed. A close-up of their daughter's face showed a lovely brown-haired girl with winsome eyes.

You couldn't look at that face and not feel sympathy for her and for her family.

There was no picture of the doctor, but there was a statement from the hospital about why the girl had been denied a transplant. After reading the explanation I admitted to myself that had I been the decision maker, I would probably have made the same choice, however reluctantly. It all made sense, but at the same time, it was hard not to feel like an exception should have been made because of her youth. It's so easy to get caught up in one person's narrative and forget about all the other people affected by the decision. In this instance, the other people waiting for a kidney.

No one in the media mentioned Jared Blaine as a player in the story. The parents must have kept that to themselves.

When Logan showed up with two sandwiches and a bag of homemade cookies, I didn't hesitate to drop what I was doing and join him on my deck for lunch. The sun was peeking through some wispy clouds, there was a warm breeze drifting across the water, and no one was shooting at us. Life was good.

I devoured my sandwich and started on my first cookie before telling him about the visit from the Blaines. I knew that telling him the Blaines thought their son was being held hostage was going to ruin the pleasant moment we were enjoying. As anticipated, Logan was irate.

"Huh! Those poor people. Someone is stringing them along, and . . ."

"I know. I feel so bad about not telling them the full story, but I'm not even sure they would believe me."

Logan grabbed another cookie, chewing rapidly, as if angry at the cookie. "I've been thinking about the backpack. In spite of what Fiona told you, isn't it possible one of the rescue team guys mentioned it to someone?"

"You mean they told someone about the crazy American who thought she'd come upon a dead hiker?"

"Yeah, something like that."

"That I can see, but why mention the backpack?"

"Because that was part of your story."

"But why lie to Fiona?"

"Maybe they were embarrassed about making fun of you in front of their drinking buddies. That's one scenario."

It made some sense, but still seemed unlikely. I couldn't picture Allen caring if he sounded rude or insensitive. "I don't think so . . ."

"What about Keith then?" Logan said. "You say you didn't tell him about the backpack, but he might have used his charm or his connections to learn more about Blaine and his disappearance. Maybe he already knew who Blaine was and why he was there. There has to be a reason he keeps popping up."

"You don't think it's just my feminine charm?" I snatched the last cookie out of Logan's hand. We were fighting over it when my cell rang. It was Sophie. Logan used the distraction to grab what remained of the cookie and popped it in his mouth. "Damn," I said. They were really good cookies.

"Is that the way you answer your phone these days?" Sophie asked.

"Sorry, I was commenting on something Logan just did."

"Well, put that aside, okay? I have something you need to know. In fact, put me on speaker."

I switched to speaker, and Logan pulled his chair closer.

"Conrad didn't show up to work today," Sophie said. "And he isn't answering his phone."

"I was going to call him as soon as we finished lunch," I said. My noon deadline was up, and I'd wanted to check with Conrad one last time before talking to Ben about what he'd told me.

"Well, no one here is particularly worried, but I am. For

obvious reasons. I can't get away or I'd run by and see if he is okay myself. If I give you his address can the two of you check him out?"

We quickly agreed.

Ben called before I even managed to put down the phone. I told him we were on the way to see whether my contact at the "Say No to Chimeras" group was okay and that I needed to talk to him about the Blaines. He didn't question why we were concerned about Conrad. He simply asked for his address and said he would meet us there. He was a quick study.

We left immediately, but Ben beat us to Conrad's condo. He was waiting for us on the sidewalk in front of the string of brightly colored, connected units that formed a "U" with an expansive walkway down the middle. Each unit entrance was separated by a single car garage. Conrad's unit was the second one on the left. It was painted bright green, and there was a large pot filled with fragrant yellow and pink flowers next to his front door. I rang the doorbell and heard it echo inside. When nothing happened, I tried knocking. Still nothing.

"Now what?" Logan asked. It was obvious that having Ben there limited our options. Or maybe it expanded them. It depended on his approach.

"Let's see if there are any windows around back," Ben suggested. He took the lead and we followed him along the side of the condo. The back of Conrad's unit was enclosed by a wood fence with a gate that opened onto a path leading to a glass sliding door. There were windows on both sides of the door, but they were covered by wood slat blinds. The door, however, had no curtains or blinds.

"Is it okay if I take a peek inside?" I asked Ben. I would have to go through the gate to get there. Would Ben consider that trespassing?

"Someone from his office did ask you to check on him," Ben said.

"I take it that's a 'yes.'"

Ben briefly hesitated before gesturing for me to go ahead.

It took me a minute to figure out the gate mechanism, but when I did, it opened with a loud squeak. We went inside, me in the lead, Logan right behind me, and Ben bringing up the rear.

Most of the plants in the yard looked in need of water, but there was a tomato plant in a small planter box that I immediately coveted. It was covered with a cascade of red cherry tomatoes just begging to be picked.

I put my hand over my eyes to block out the sunlight and peered in through the glass door. Logan stood to my right, mimicking my hand-over-eyes stance to get a better look inside. There was a kitchen counter to the right with a view into the living room on the left. A lamp lay on the floor next to an end table in the living room.

"Damn," Logan and I said simultaneously.

"The lamp?" I asked. He nodded.

Ben stepped around me and tried the door. We were all surprised when it slid open. "Conrad," he yelled. "Anyone home?"

There was no answer.

"Stay here," Ben ordered. Logan and I nodded as if in agreement, but there was no way I was going to wait outside while Ben searched the condo. We gave Ben a few steps head start before following.

It was clear immediately that there had been a fight in the living room. And . . . there was blood on the floor between the living room and the kitchen.

Ben motioned us back and drew out his gun. But he didn't need it.

We found Conrad in the kitchen, unconscious but still alive. He had been badly beaten. Even so he had managed to drag himself from the living room to the kitchen, maybe hoping to reach his cell phone which was on the counter.

Ben immediately called for an ambulance and told us to stay

put and not touch anything while he searched the rest of the condo to make sure no one was there. This time we stayed put.

The ambulance was there in under ten minutes. Ben had them come in through the back so as not to disturb the crime scene. After Conrad was loaded onto a gurney and taken away, Ben turned to me and said, "You may have saved his life."

"Sophie may have saved his life," I corrected. "I may have endangered it."

"You know who did this?"

"No, but you should definitely question members of the 'Say No to Chimeras' group. Conrad was going to ask around to see if one or more of them was responsible for searching my office and locker, maybe even for shooting at me."

"I thought you were keeping a low profile?"

"He came to see me; I didn't go to him. Apparently, some of their members think I know where Jared is and believe that I may even have his research data."

Ben didn't look happy. "Why didn't you tell me sooner?"

"Well, I promised Conrad that I would give him some time to check on his own."

"We thought he would learn more that way," Logan said, trying to assume some of the blame. I appreciated his gesture, but I knew I was the one ultimately responsible for my decisions.

Ben looked down at the blood on the kitchen floor. "Maybe he did learn something. Let's just hope he regains consciousness and can tell us what."

"There's one more thing you need to know," I said. I knew I had to tell him about the Blaines before anything else went sideways. We went back the way we had come in. Ben had called in what had happened, and there was an investigative team on its way. While he waited for them to show, I quickly filled him in on the Blaines and their belief that their son was being held hostage.

As Ben listened, he kept shaking his head. "I can't believe I didn't pick up on any of this when I talked to them," he said when I had finished.

"They're scared," I said. "Really scared. They took the warning not to talk to the police seriously."

"Still—"

"The worst part is that I couldn't tell them the truth. I feel terrible about lying to them."

"You didn't actually lie to them," Logan said. "Just omitted some information."

Whether it was an outright lie or a lie of omission, it didn't make me feel any better about what I had done. And it didn't keep me from feeling guilty as hell about Conrad.

back to high school

We called Sophie on the way back to the marina. She was upset about Conrad and felt like it was all her fault. We argued back and forth over what share of the blame each of us was responsible for before Logan finally said, "Enough already. We can allocate blame later. What we have to do now is figure out how to keep this from happening to anyone else."

Sophie said she would join us this evening to talk about whether there was anything else we could do to sort things out. Meanwhile, she had the onerous task of telling everyone at her office about what had happened to Conrad. Then she was going to check at the hospital to see how he was doing.

When we arrived at the marina neither of us got out of the car, instead we sat there staring straight ahead. I always enjoy looking at boats. Power boats, working boats, but most of all sailboats. I'm quickly transported by imagination to being on the open water, the arc of a sail while beating into the wind. Sometimes I visualize what it must be like to haul pots on a crab boat or to navigate a tug pulling a barge. Each maritime experience is a different world, a snapshot in time to be savored. But today, I wasn't seeing anything or thinking anything; I was simply staring into space.

"You want to go back to your office?" Logan asked finally.

"No, what about you? What do you want to do?"

"I don't know. But I don't think I'm going to be able to concentrate on reading student essays given what happened this morning."

"I feel the same. I know we told Ben we were coming back here, and we're supposed to step back and let the police do their job. But . . . there is one thing I've been thinking about doing," I said slowly. "Something that I doubt is on the police radar."

"Which is?"

"We could talk to Jack and Evie Davidson, the couple who wanted Jared to experiment on their daughter, Melissa."

"You think they would know something about Jared's disappearance? Or that they might actually be involved? After all this time?" His tone told me that he thought I was suggesting something as unlikely as finding a swimming pool on Mars.

"I agree it's a longshot," I admitted. "But they obviously investigated him and his work, so maybe there's something they could tell us that would be helpful."

Logan chewed on the idea for what seemed like an hour but was probably less than a minute. "Would you approach them directly?" He sounded hesitant.

I had been contemplating possible ways to introduce myself to them. "No, not initially at least. Maybe talk with them about something else first. Feel out the situation. Then we can decide how—or if—we should bring up the subject." "So how would we go about it?"

"Well, she's a teacher at that middle school we pass all the time on the way to the farmers' market. And he works for a tech company. I say we start with her." I smiled. "Don't we have a niece who is coming to live with us? It would be a good idea to check out the school, right?"

"Seems a little farfetched," Logan said. He definitely didn't seem to be warming to the idea.

"We don't have to make up a story. Well, not much of a story anyway. But we've got to have a reason for stopping by the school."

Logan and I stared at the boats in the marina a few more minutes without speaking. There were two crows dive bombing a seagull who seemed determined to hold his ground. But it was a losing battle against two determined crows.

"What if we were reporters?" Logan said. "What could we be investigating?"

"A good school for our niece." We both laughed.

"Okay, I'm in." He sounded more resigned than enthusiastic. "But I want it on the record that it was *your* idea."

"Actually, I think we should keep this *off* the record. No one needs to know—unless we discover something relevant, of course."

While I drove, Logan researched the school on his iPhone. He learned that they had been in the news recently for a new STEM mentoring program they were piloting to get more students interested in science. Evie Davidson's name didn't come up as one of the teachers involved, but it was an excuse to check out the school.

"Maybe you should be who you are," I said, "a college professor interested in making sure kids get a good education."

"What a novel idea."

"Sometimes the truth is a good option."

Logan sighed. "There goes my one chance to be a reporter. But I think you're right."

The school was an old brick building long past its prime. Still, the lawn was nicely trimmed, and mature trees added a touch of stateliness and a sense of stability to the setting. There was an almost full parking lot around back. As we wended our way through the lot, we speculated about whether teachers or students were driving the junkers we were seeing and who was responsible for the occasional electric car. There was also one pink car that we decided belonged to a teacher who supplemented her salary by moonlighting for Mary Kay. We finally found a space and pulled into it.

It was near the end of the school day. There was no one around, but there was a camera over the entrance at the rear of the building.

"Think we need to go around front?" I asked.

"Let's find out."

We went up the back steps and through the unlocked door into a long corridor with tiny square windows in scratched wood doors. It looked so familiar. But as we peeked into a couple of classrooms, we noted that one thing had changed. Gone were the old-fashioned desks we remembered. The tables and chairs in these room looked like something you might find in a business setting. In one room students sat in chairs that formed a large U facing a teacher at a whiteboard in the front of the room. Another room had an empty rectangular table in the middle with a few easy chairs off to the side. A boy slouched in one of them, working his iPad.

We went around a corner and came to a row of grey metal lockers. "I thought schools had done away with lockers," Logan said.

"No locks," I observed. "Maybe they don't use them."

"So how does it improve safety if they're still here but not assigned to anyone?"

"Beats me." I suddenly remembered running from one class to another with a quick stop at my locker to drop off one set of books and pick up another. Even with a good backpack I couldn't imagine lugging all those books around.

A woman dressed in a beige sweater and slacks hurried in our direction. Her brown hair was tucked neatly behind her ears.

She looked pleasant enough, but there was something about her manner that suggested both authority and alarm.

"Can I help you?" she asked loudly.

Her tone strongly implied we had broken a rule by coming in through the back. If so, they should be more careful about locking their doors.

"Yes," Logan said in his most beguiling voice. "I teach at the university. I've read about your STEM mentoring program and wondered if it would be possible to talk to a few of the teachers about how it's going."

"Could I see some ID?" I noted she did not say "please."

We both instantly reached for our IDs, but as I did so I felt like telling her that she should have called security instead of confronting us on her own. She was lucky our subterfuge didn't have evil intent.

She looked at our IDs and then at us. Apparently satisfied, she asked, "Would you mind telling me what your specific interest is in our program?" There was a touch of pride in the way she referred to "our" program.

"I like to encourage students to consider careers in teaching, so when I hear about something innovative, I try to find out as much as I can. To get them excited about the possibilities."

That seemed a little thin to me, but apparently the word "innovative" combined with Logan's innate charm was sufficient to win the day. She said that classes would be out soon, and a number of teachers gathered in the teacher's lounge to chat and grab a cup of tea or coffee before returning to their classrooms to do whatever needed to be done before calling it a day. She offered to show us to the lounge.

"And are you a teacher here?" Logan asked. "No, I'm the Vice Principal."

"So, you have a pretty good feel for the overall success of the program."

"Yes, we are very pleased with how things are going." She looked both pleased and proud. "Especially with the number of girls in the program."

When we reached the lounge, the first thing that caught my attention was a wall filled with pictures. These were the school's teachers, posted alphabetically. Evie Davidson had smiled directly into the camera, her light brown hair attractively cut to frame high cheekbones and a sharp jawline.

"I think I recognize her," I said to the Vice Principal, pointing at Evie's picture.

"Evie? An excellent teacher."

I hesitated, then went for broke. "Weren't she and her husband in the news a few years back?"

The Vice Principal frowned. "It was an unfortunate incident." Her tone suggested it was not one she wanted to talk about.

"They lost their daughter, didn't they?" Logan pressed, ignoring her hint to let the topic go. "She was refused a transplant, as I remember."

"That's correct." The Vice Principal started to turn away, but Logan quickly added,

"And my recollection of the newspaper coverage was that the doctor and the hospital involved were fairly coldhearted in their decision-making process. At least that's how it seemed to me at the time."

The Vice Principal took a deep breath before responding. "Evie and her husband tried everything they could to save their child. Everything. But no one was willing to help. The family was devastated." She paused, and before I got a chance to ask what she meant by emphasizing "everything," a bell rang, a loud, hard sound, and the room was almost instantly filled with chatter and end-of-the-day ebullience.

Our chance to question the Vice Principal further came to an end. She waved over a young man and introduced him as one of the teachers participating in the mentoring program and explained to him that we were interested in learning more about it. Then she immediately departed. Unfortunately, the teacher was in a hurry and turned us over to another teacher who was also in a hurry. She gave us a few minutes before excusing herself. I kept looking around for Evie Davidson but didn't see her. After about ten minutes the teachers drifted away with their afternoon cups of tea and coffee, their voices fading, like the volume on a radio slowly being turned down until nothing but a low-level hum remained. The only thing we had to show for our visit was a slightly improved understanding of the school's STEM mentoring program. As for our actual purpose, we were none the wiser.

We briefly considered trying to look for Evie's classroom before reluctantly concluding that our whole trip had been lame. What were we thinking? No one was going to tell us anything we hadn't already read in the papers. And if we did manage to talk with Evie, it was going to be extremely difficult to broach the subject. Nevertheless, I was glad we had come. I felt sorry for Evie's loss and was pleased to have seen the smiling picture of her on the wall. I wanted to believe she had moved on and hadn't just faked a smile for the camera.

As we got back in the car my phone went off. It was Sophie. She was just leaving the hospital. Conrad was still unconscious. "Want to meet for Happy Hour?" She didn't have to ask twice.

Happy Hour wasn't very happy for us. Sophie was still feeling guilty about Conrad. She and Logan were worried about me. And I was feeling like I'd just lost a game because the rules weren't clear, and I didn't even know who the other players were. I didn't like being in the dark and out of control.

We hadn't been there more than five minutes when my phone did its thing. Everyone in the bar turned to check out who had the stupid frog party ringtone. I was considering not answering when I realized it was my mother. At least I could keep it short by telling her I was with friends in a bar. "Bryn, thank god you're there," she said. She sounded very upset.

"What's wrong, mother?"

"We were burgled," she said. "Your father is beside himself."

"Oh no. Was much taken?"

"No, that's the strange thing. But they broke a window and made a mess."

"Was the alarm on?" I had to ask. Dylan and I had purchased an alarm system for them, but we were having a hard time getting them to use it.

"That isn't the worst thing," she said, sidestepping my question.

"What *is* the worst thing?" I didn't like the idea that there was something even worse than my parents being burgled.

"They left a picture of Noah and Emma in the playground at school taped to the mirror in the dining room." Her voice was shaking. "Next to a note addressed to us."

My stomach muscles felt the impact before I actually processed what she was saying. "Oh no." I could barely speak.

"What did the note say?"

"Bryn . . ., we're so scared."

I didn't want to admit that I was scared too. "What did the note say, Mother?" I somehow managed to keep my voice calm even though I guessed what was coming.

"It says: 'Tell your daughter that we want what she took. We'll be in touch.'" She paused, then asked, "Does that make any sense to you?"

I didn't know how to respond, how to reassure her. I flashed on Blaine's body at the bottom of the ravine and the goldfish impaled by my letter opener. These people weren't playing games. I needed to come clean with Dylan and Angelina, explain what was going on. If anything happened to Noah and Emma, I would never forgive myself.

"You've notified the police?"

"Yes, they should be here any minute."

"I'm going to call Ben," I said. It was all I could think of to do. "And I'll be there as soon as I can."

CHAPTER 23

the eye in the woods

Logan drove. I was too upset to be trusted behind the wheel. Sophie was in the back seat. When I couldn't get my brother on the phone, I was even more upset. "Why isn't he answering?" I asked. It was a rhetorical question, but both Logan and Sophie responded.

"Maybe they went out to dinner," Sophie offered.

"Maybe your parents called them, and they're on the way over there."

"In either case," I said, "he could answer his damn phone." I knew I was being irrational, but then, that was how I felt. It was one thing to put myself at risk, but another to put my family in jeopardy. How could things have escalated to this point?

Why wouldn't they—whoever "they" were—believe me when I said that I didn't have Jared's research? What was it going to take to convince them to leave me and my family alone?

When we arrived, every light in the house was on. Dylan's car was in the driveway, and I saw Dylan peek out the window. Noah was standing beside him. Thank god.

A police car pulled up behind us, but we didn't hang around to talk to them. All three of us made a beeline for the front door. When I saw Emma and knew that both children were safe and sound, my heart almost returned to its normal rate. Almost. Noah and Emma came running over. "Auntie Bryn," they yelled, hurtling themselves into my open arms.

"Hey, kiddos," I said. "It's good to see you." They didn't know just how good.

Dylan joined us at the same time the police knocked on the door. He went past me to answer it, but Logan was already there. My mother and father appeared, with Angelina bringing up the rear. It was suddenly chaotic in the tiny foyer as everyone seemed to be talking at once.

The police finally got us to sort ourselves out. My parents and I went with them into the living room while everyone else was asked to go into the kitchen and wait. Noah and Emma were subdued at the sight of officers in uniforms. They obviously knew something unusual was going on. Dylan and Angelina were going to have some explaining to do to keep their kids from becoming overly anxious about the burglary. I was confident they would know how to have that conversation, but I wasn't sure what they were going to say and do once they became aware of the full scope of the problem. How do you keep kids safe if you don't tell them they are in danger? And how do you explain to a five-year-old the difference between being careful and not letting fear dominate their life? I wasn't even sure I knew how to do that.

Ben arrived just as my parents were showing the officers the note and telling them about the picture. He introduced himself to the officers and explained that he was working on a case that the break-in might be related to. For a few seconds it seemed as though there could be some tension over who was in charge, but when Ben told the officers to proceed and he would observe, everyone seemed satisfied.

"If they didn't take anything," one of the officers said, "but they want 'something' back, then . . .?" He looked at me. "Are you the one the note refers to?"

My parents turned toward me. Ben, too, turned to look at me. The other officer's head swiveled in my direction. It was my show.

"Yes, I know what they were looking for," I admitted. "The problem is, I don't have it." Everyone waited. I couldn't think of anything to say but the truth. "They think I have a laptop that contains research from a company called Humanity Health Group, a subsidiary of NorPac."

"But why would they think that?" my father asked, sounding truly puzzled.

"Because I, ah, ran across the scientist involved when I was in Scotland. And now he's gone missing." It would have been a lot easier if I had told my parents the whole story to begin with. But I hadn't wanted to upset them. And look where that had landed me.

"Has anyone but you handled the note?" Ben interrupted.

"Well," mother hesitated. "Dylan, I think."

"If you don't mind," Ben said as he put on some gloves. "I'd like to have this tested for fingerprints." Mother thrust it at him as if it were on fire. The officers exchanged glances but didn't say anything.

Ben turned to the officers. "After you've finished questioning everyone and have taken a look around, why don't we talk. I think I can clarify a few things." There were obviously a few jurisdictional issues to settle, but the officers seemed to respond positively to Ben's demeanor and authority.

The officers went with my parents to check out the broken window and assess what there was to assess. Since my parents didn't think anything had been disturbed elsewhere in the house, it appeared as though whoever had broken in hadn't bothered with a search. So, there wasn't a lot the police could do. But they had been called to check out a break-in, and they had to go through the motions.

When the officers were finished looking around, Ben went outside to talk with them. Meanwhile, I tried to calm everyone down, even though I wasn't feeling so calm myself. Logan took Noah and Emma into the living room to watch TV while the rest of the grownups huddled in the kitchen.

Dylan ripped into me the instant the kids were out of earshot. "What the hell are you mixed up in?"

"It's not her fault," Sophie said, defending me like she had since we were kids.

"I don't care whose fault it is," Angelina said. "I just want to make sure our children are safe."

"That's what I want too," I assured them.

Ben came into the kitchen and motioned for me to come with him. "Bryn, you and I need to talk." He looked around at my agitated family and added, "Then I'll come back and we can discuss what you should do to protect yourselves, okay?"

We went out onto the front porch. Ben leaned against the railing while I stood before him like a child about to be scolded by a parent. "Bryn, are you absolutely sure you've told me everything?"

"Yes, I have. Everything. And I've imagined every possible scenario about what could have happened to Blaine and his research. None of it makes any sense. Take his research, for instance. Even if he didn't have his laptop or tablet with him on the trail that day, he wouldn't have left them lying around back at the inn. And if it had been me, I'd have put the data on a thumb. But his computer, his tablet, any backup—they all seem to have disappeared. *Someone* took everything.

"The question is why anyone would think I was the one responsible, why I would have taken his research in the first place. The only possibly is that the killer didn't have time to go through his pack before I came down the hill. If they were hiding in the trees, maybe they couldn't see what, if anything, I removed and assumed the worst. But if that's the case, then why didn't they go after me while I was still in Scotland? And if it isn't Blaine's killer who is trying to get the data from me, then what makes someone else assume I have whatever it is they are looking for?"

"And even if they thought you'd taken something from the backpack, why would they think you were hanging onto it instead of turning it in?"

"Who knows? Maybe they think I want to sell the data, and they want to get their hands on it before that happens. Or maybe they think that I'm part of the 'Say No' group and assume I want to make sure it never sees the light of day. Maybe I should announce that I'm against chimera research and that I've already destroyed Blaine's research."

"No, I don't think that's a good idea. It's best to keep telling the truth. That you don't have it and never have had it."

"But what about my family?"

"The fact that someone has threatened them, and you still maintain you don't have the research should make your denial more credible."

"Why not contact me directly?"

"I'm sure they will, probably soon. They're trying to soften you up by putting pressure on you through your family."

"Well, they're doing a damn fine job."

"Okay, let's go back in there and see if we can encourage caution without scaring them too much."

"Good luck doing that with Angelina."

Ben stopped me as I was about to go back inside. "And that goes for you, too. You've got to be careful. Never go anywhere alone. And as soon as they contact you, let me know. Understand?"

I was torn between appreciating his concern and being irritated by the fact that he apparently thought I needed a lecture. I'm not adverse to taking a few risks, but these people were way above my paygrade. There was no question about it, I was definitely going to play it safe, and then some.

It took all of Ben's authority and diplomacy to get my family to listen and to agree on a few cautionary ground rules. At one point, Logan poked his head in the room and asked us to keep it down. I could hear the television blaring in the background. He'd probably been turning it up louder and louder to distract the kids from the animated discussion in the kitchen.

The bottom line was simple—until someone contacted me

there was nothing any of us could do except obey the ground rules. There were five basic rules when outside the home: Don't wander off alone. Be constantly aware of your surroundings. Don't assume that daylight made you safer. Keep car doors locked, even when in a gas station. And, most important, keep a cell phone with Ben's number handy. In addition, there were some "at-home" rules: Lock all doors and windows. Turn on alarms. Don't answer the door unless you know who is there. And keep a cell phone with Ben's number handy.

My father told Ben that he had a rifle and asked if he recommended getting a handgun. Ben said "no" and explained how most handguns end up being used against their owners. He did tell my mother that she might want to keep her pepper spray handy and to make sure she knew which way to point it. I didn't think he really expected her to use it, but I could tell she found it reassuring to have something she could do on her own. For once Dylan didn't pretend he had all the answers. He seemed to respect Ben's expertise. And having his kids threatened undoubtedly made him especially receptive to suggestions about how to keep everyone safe.

By the time Ben had gone through the "rules" several times and answered all our questions as best he could, my family appeared not only subdued but appropriately wary. I felt guilty as hell and hoped that I would soon get the opportunity to convince whoever had done this that they were going after the wrong person.

Logan, Sophie and I were headed back to get Sophie's car when she got a call from the hospital. Conrad had regained consciousness. Technically visiting hours were over, but Conrad was asking for Sophie, and the nurse said she thought it would help calm him if Sophie could come by.

When we arrived at the hospital it took a little doing to convince the nurse that all three of us should be let in to see Conrad. She only gave in when she got an urgent call to attend to another patient. She probably knew that as soon as she was gone we would go in with or without permission.

Conrad looked terrible. Between the bandages and the bruises, he could have been an accident victim on some ER drama. His eyes were closed when we entered, and when he opened them and saw me, he said, "Not *you*." Sophie quickly stepped up next to his bed and took his hand.

"Hey, Con, you look terrible," she said. He managed a weak smile.

"I came earlier to see how you were doing."

"The nurse told me."

"The whole office is thinking of you and sending well wishes your way."

"Thank you." He closed his eyes, and for a minute I thought he was going to fall back into a coma.

"Do you want me to come back tomorrow?" Sophie asked gently.

No, I silently screamed, I wanted to hear what he had to say tonight. Right now. Before anything else happened. But I kept my mouth shut. I can be persistent and demanding, but I'm not totally insensitive.

"No," he said, opening his eyes. "I want to tell you what happened."

"Shouldn't you be talking to the police?" Sophie asked.

Whose side was she on, anyway?!

"I don't want anyone else to get hurt," he said.

"Do you know who did this to you?" she asked.

"No, they were wearing masks."

"Do you know what they wanted?"

"Yes." He paused. I was leaning forward on the balls of my feet, willing him to talk. I noticed that Logan was also leaning forward. We were like two vultures waiting to pounce.

"What did they say?" Sophie prompted.

"They wanted Blaine's data. They seemed convinced that

Bryn had given it to us and that we were going to destroy it. Publicly. To make a point."

"And what did you tell them?"

"That we didn't have it. And that I didn't think Bryn did either. But they wouldn't believe me." His voice was growing softer, as if it was going to slowly fade away into nothingness.

"Is that why they beat you, to get you to tell the 'truth'?"

"Yes." His voice was barely audible. "They kept trying to get me to confess . . ."

"Did they say anything to indicate why they think Bryn has the data?"

"She went through his backpack . . ." He closed his eyes. His breathing seemed shallow but normal. We looked at each other.

Sophie mouthed: "Should we call the nurse?"

Logan shrugged. He didn't know. Nor did I. We were saved from having to decide by the reappearance of the nurse on her own.

"He seems to have dropped off," Sophie said.

The nurse quickly waved us back and moved in to check Conrad's vitals. She didn't say anything right away, but her features slowly seemed to relax, and I felt the tension leave my shoulders.

The nurse then ushered us out of the room. "He needs rest," she said.

"Would you tell him that any time he feels like talking to me he can call?" Sophie handed the nurse her card.

As we walked down the long corridor lined with wheelchairs and medical apparatus, Logan said, "It *does* make sense. You give the 'Say No' group the data. They prove they have it and make a show of destroying it. That's good TV. I'm sure they could get coverage for it."

"But it begs the point," I said. "I didn't know Blaine. I've never been associated with chimera research in any way. And I never had the data."

"It's that backpack evidence again," Sophie said.

"Someone saw you," Logan said. "But if it was the killer, why not challenge you right then and there?"

Yes, that was the million-dollar question. My gut had been right—there must have been someone in the woods, watching. But if they had been concerned about me taking something, why had they let me slip away? Why had they let me leave Scotland and come after me with a vengeance now? I remembered something Churchill once said: "*It is a riddle, wrapped in a mystery, inside an enigma.*" That's how this entire situation was beginning to feel.

CHAPTER 24

panic!

By the time we went back to pick up Sophie's car, followed her home and made sure she was safely locked in for the night, it was close to midnight. Logan checked his email while I drove us back to the marina. "There's a message from Gray," he said. Then, after a pause, he summarized what Gray had learned. "It seems that MedTech has openly expressed interest in chimera research, but it isn't clear whether they are negotiating for a share of the pie with NorPac or what. Bottom line is that they are doing just fine without expanding into other markets."

"They could still be the bad guys," I said.

"It's possible."

Back at the marina we headed down the dock together in silence, the sound of our footfalls unnaturally loud in the dead of night calm. For me, the marina had gone from being a welcome and interesting place to live to a sinister space filled with potential danger. As I shied away from dark corners and jumped at even familiar noises, I wondered if I would ever manage to recapture the sense of warmth and community that it once represented.

When we got to the *Carpe Diem*, there were no lights on, so I said goodbye to Logan and tiptoed over to the *Aspara*. Logan waited until I was safely aboard. Macavity was on the couch. He didn't open his eyes, but his tail flicked in greeting. Or annoyance. It was hard to say.

I was about to get undressed when I heard someone running across the *Carpe Diem*. Macavity came to full alert as I instinctively grabbed my phone to call Ben. Then someone pounded on my hatch and called, "Bryn, Bryn, are you in there? It's me, Keith."

Keith? What on earth was he doing on my boat at this hour? And why did he sound panicked?

"Come out of there," I heard Logan yell. "I'm calling the police."

No, Logan, I thought. Call first, *before* the threat. But then, Keith wasn't being secretive.

"Bryn," Keith called again. "You need to get out of here now. Do you hear me?"

"And *you* need to get off that boat *now*." Logan yelled.

I was torn. Keith was the bad guy, but he sounded sincerely upset. And Logan and Judd were right there. So, I unlocked the hatch and pulled it back.

"Thank god," Keith said. "You need to come with me. They're going to be here any minute."

"I'm not going anywhere with you," I said.

"Then . . . then . . ." He looked around. "Then untie your boat and take off," he said

"And I suppose you'll come with me."

Keith turned toward Logan. "You—what's your name?" he asked.

"Logan." For some reason Logan was also responding to what sounded like genuine urgency in Keith's demand.

Keith reached into his pocket and pulled out a gun. Before we could react, he handed it butt first to Logan. "Take this and come with us, okay? But we have to act now."

By then Judd was on deck and trying to take everything in while still half asleep.

"Look," Keith said, waving at Judd. "You come too. Bring the whole damn marina if you want, but we need to make tracks fast." He looked from me to Logan to Judd. "The guys on the way here are dangerous. Very dangerous. I'll explain once we are out of here."

"Okay," I said, making a decision I hoped I wouldn't regret. "Come on, Logan, help me untie and let's go." I looked over at Judd. "Do you want to stay here or come with us?"

"He should come," Keith said. "They know where you've been tied up."

"I'm not leaving the *Carpe Diem*," Judd said.

"Keith, you help Judd untie," Logan said. "I'll go with Bryn. You can follow in the *Carpe Diem*."

Keith didn't argue. He obviously wanted us out of there more than he wanted to do it his way. Within a few minutes the two boats were chugging out of the marina and headed west toward the industrial part of the Ship Canal. I didn't actually have a plan. All I wanted was a marina where we could disappear for a while so we had time to hear Keith out.

"What do you think, Logan? Where should we go?"

He suggested a marina he knew that had gated docks that were locked up at night. "We can stop there and figure things out. They might expect us to head straight for the locks, so I don't think we should do that. We'd be trapped."

"I agree, let's stop and reconnoiter. We can make plans based on what Keith tells us." I paused. "Still have his gun?" "Yes." Logan pulled it out of his jacket pocket.

"Is it loaded?" It had crossed my mind that the gun gambit had been just that, a trick. But when Logan checked, there were bullets. "That doesn't mean it's in working order," I said.

"No, but I'm not going to check that out at the moment."

"We need to be careful," I said. "This could all be a trick."

"A pretty elaborate one," Logan said. "He could have ambushed us. Or set the *Aspara* adrift and shot you when you came out to see what was happening."

"He sounded scared," I said. "But a good con man knows how to play his victims."

"Tell me again who you think he works for."

"I'm not sure. Maybe a rival company. Someone who thinks the information might be worth something. Maybe he was the hit man. I just don't know."

"But you never told him about the backpack."

"No, I didn't."

"So, if he knows about it . . ."

"He thinks he saw me take it. He doesn't realize I only removed a business card from the pack."

"Or someone else told him you took the pack." Judd frowned. "So, friend or enemy, that's a tough one."

"And who are we running away from? And…" Something occurred to me that I should have thought of immediately. "What if they're tracking my cell phone?" I took it out and held it up as if we could tell by looking at it if it was betraying us.

"Turn off your phone," Logan ordered. "Now."

I quickly turned it off. "Think that will do it?"

"I don't know. We can talk about it after we tie up." Logan smiled. "Unless you want to toss it overboard now to be on the safe side."

As frightened as I was, that was something I wasn't willing to do…yet.

Both Judd and I broke the law by failing to turn on our running lights. I was prepared to plead ignorance if stopped. It seemed well worth the risk of a fine to avoid being easily spotted from shore.

When Logan's phone rang, we both jumped. "It's Judd," he said. He listened for about fifteen seconds, then hung up and switched off his phone. "We're supposed to turn off our phones, so we can only be tracked to where we are now. Unless they have really sophisticated equipment, which Keith doesn't think they have."

"That's reassuring."

Logan rolled his eyes. "Let's hope he's right."

When we reached the marina, Logan had first thought of, we turned in toward land, looking for empty slips far enough out in the marina to accommodate our keel depth. The *Aspara* draws about six feet, the *Carpe Diem* about the same even though it's longer and wider. Unfortunately, there didn't seem to be any empty slips far enough out that were close to each other. Nor were there any boats large enough to mask our presence from someone searching from shore. We turned back and continued on.

Our second stop was more promising. The marina was a large one with a combination of pleasure and working boat tenants. The docks weren't gated, but there were a number of large boats, good camouflage for two boats hoping to disappear into the night.

We were in luck. There was a finger float about halfway in with spaces on either side empty. Our masts would be visible to someone who knew what they were looking for, but we could probably count on some lead time before we were spotted. And if we'd managed to get away before they'd arrived at the marina, they might not even know in which direction we had gone. Especially if they hadn't been tracking our phones. With luck, it wouldn't be easy to track us down either by land or via water.

I pulled the *Aspara* into the slip closest to shore, and the *Carpe Diem* pulled in on the other side. As soon as the two boats were secured, Logan and I joined Keith and Judd on the *Carpe Diem*. I went in first, looking at Judd for any cue that said, "run for it." But he was busy making coffee. I took that as a sign he'd been satisfied with whatever story Keith had told him.

Keith was seated on the couch. His head was resting on the back cushion. He looked tired rather than relaxed. Logan took a seat at the end of the dinette across from the couch, and I slid in next to him.

"Do you take cream or sugar?" Judd asked Keith as if this was a social event rather than some kind of crisis.

"No, black. Thanks." Keith straightened up and looked at me. "I owe you an explanation," he began. I was tempted to make some cutting remark, but I couldn't think of any, so I waited for him to continue. "I'm not who you think I am," Keith said.

"It depends on who you think I think you are," I commented, feeling initially like I'd just said something clever, but realizing after it was out that it had been pretty lame.

Keith smiled. "Well, let me say first of all that I didn't kill Jared Blaine. Nor was I in the area when it happened. Some people I'm, ah, associated with, monitor police calls. When you contacted the Mountain Rescue Team, they called the police. It's procedure." He paused as Judd handed him a cup of coffee. There was a small pull-down table at the end of the couch. Keith took a sip and placed the cup on the table.

"So, the people you are 'associated' with knew who Blaine was," Logan said.

"Yes. The research he was involved with is quite controversial in our corner of the world. Partly because of our local lab. Although our researchers are more regulated than yours. And we've spent more time addressing the ethical issues."

"Are you associated with some international network of chimera protesters?" I asked. That seemed unlikely to me, but I had to ask.

Keith smiled again. "No, I'm afraid my associates are interested more in profit than in saving lives or preventing the creation of monsters."

Fiona was right, he was one of the bad guys. But if so, why was he trying to help me? Or was he?

"Look, I'm sorry you ended up in the middle of this. I just hope by warning you tonight that I haven't blown my cover." As if he was suddenly aware of what he had done, he looked at Logan and asked, "How do I get back to the marina from here at this hour without calling a cab?"

"It's a long walk," Logan said.

"He can borrow one of our folding bikes," Judd offered.

Obviously, Judd was on Keith's side. "He could make it back in about 20-30 minutes, don't you think?"

"First," I interrupted, "I want to know who you *claim* to work for."

"*Claim*?" Keith seemed amused by the thought that I wasn't about to accept anything he told us at face value.

"Yes, not that I'd believe anything you said at this point."

"Look, I'm sorry you're involved. And, well, this is going to sound a bit dramatic." He looked from me to Logan to Judd and back to me. "And I'm not supposed to tell anyone, but under the circumstances I think you have to know. What I'm asking is that you keep it to yourselves. Can you do that?" He looked from me to Logan to Judd and back again. For whatever reason, we all nodded "yes."

"I started working for a branch of Interpol about fifteen years ago."

"What?" I said louder than I'd intended. Keith held up his hand for me to wait until he finished.

"We monitor potentially dangerous groups and movements. I can't really say more than that. They approached me originally because of my family connections. My family dabbles in a variety of illegal activities, anything to make a buck. They aren't big time, but they do have links with what is sometimes referred to as the 'criminal underworld.' And, in spite of a few minor discretions when I was younger, I had managed to stay out of the family business. But there was always a lot of pressure to become part of the family team." He took a sip of coffee.

"Each of us is stuck with the family we're born into. And sometimes they aren't people you would choose to associate with . . . but they are still family. There's an emotional bond. I didn't want to see them go to jail, but I didn't necessarily want them to succeed in some of their, ah, endeavors. So, when Interpol recruited me, I made a deal. I'm only useful as an informant if my family remains free to continue with business as usual. They are my 'cover.'"

He looked around as if trying to judge whether we were buying his story. "This has been a difficult call for me. But there are people a lot worse than my family." I tried to keep my face neutral, but Logan looked skeptical. Judd, to my surprise, seemed to be accepting what Keith was saying.

"When Blaine's laptop went missing," Keith continued, "a lot of interested parties got excited. Someone approached one of my family members and 'sold' them the information about what had happened to the laptop. He said that you, Bryn, had removed it from his backpack."

"But how did he know that unless . . ."

"He claimed the two of them had been hiking together when Blaine fell and hit his head on a boulder. He said he was going to call the police, but he didn't want to get involved."

"But this mysterious person didn't mind getting involved with your family's 'organization'?"

"He had no qualms about making money off of Blaine's death. Nor did my family. They didn't question whether his claim that it had been an accident was true or not. They didn't care. All they wanted was the data so they could sell it before someone made it to the market with similar research."

"It's really worth that much?" Logan asked.

"That's what they say."

"Do you know the name of the informant?"

"I wish I did, but I don't. The family isn't entirely open with details. It's a need-to-know climate."

"Does your family trade in illegal organ sales?" I asked. I was starting to put the pieces together, *if* Keith was to be believed.

"It's an ugly business," Keith acknowledged. "People die who shouldn't. The wealthy buy what they want. Sometimes organs are harvested from unwilling donors. It's not a world where normal rules apply. My family dabbles in the trade, but there are much bigger players."

"So, this alleged fellow hiker goes to your family and sells them information that is false. And they believe him."

"Yes, even after I assured them that you didn't have the laptop or any devices containing Blaine's research."

"And how did you know that?"

"You did quite a bit of talking about what had happened when we had drinks after the incident." Keith smiled again. Whether at the memory of our evening or his skill in prying information out of me I wasn't sure.

"But then you followed me to the US," I pointed out.

"If you hadn't become involved with the 'Say No to Chimeras' group, things would have been okay. But that just made my family believe that I had been wrong about you. They directed me to keep pressuring you to give up the data. And Interpol wants to make sure the data doesn't fall into the wrong hands. I've kept looking, but I still don't know what happened to that damn laptop, nor to the tablet, or whatever he had his research stored on."

"So, did you break into my office and locker and my parents' house? Did you leave the note and the picture?" I was starting to get angry.

"No, but I admit I knew it was going to happen. I couldn't stop it, but I've been trying to make sure no one gets hurt."

"What about the threat to my niece and nephew?"

"When they want information, they always try to find leverage. With you, Noah and Emma are . . ."

"Leverage?"

"That sounds cold. But, yes, they know you care about them and will do anything to protect them."

"Then why didn't they follow up and contact me? Why the panic tonight?"

"They're getting impatient. Worried that someone may get to you first. So, it was decided that they should pick you up and make you talk."

"That's doesn't sound good," Logan said.

"No, it isn't," Keith concluded. "They're greedy. And they can be ruthless." He finished his coffee. "Now, I'd better be getting back. I'm not parked too near the marina, but I wouldn't want them finding my car."

Judd jumped up. "I'll get the bike."

"I'll draw you a map," Logan offered, getting out a piece of paper.

"What now?" I asked.

"You stay put. The three of you stay together and out of sight. Pick up some burner phones just in case they try to trace you through your cell phones." He took out a card and wrote a number on it. "This is a safe phone. For now. Call me when you get your phones. And let me know if you go somewhere else."

"I'll need to let Ben know where I am," I said.

"Your detective friend?"

"Yes."

"You trust him?"

"Absolutely."

Keith seemed to consider. "Why don't you give me your cell. I'll make sure it gets to Ben. If they try calling you, he might be able to track them down through it. Unfortunately, I can't give them up without blowing my cover; he'll have to find them on his own. And they don't use me for muscle, so I won't necessarily be in the loop when they make their next move. Tonight was a fluke —I just happened to be there when they made the decision to come after you. But if I do learn anything that puts you in imme-diate danger, I'll be in touch."

The thought that someone would sic "muscle" on me sent a shiver down my back.

"And I'll let my employers know that Ben is a potential safe contact. But you stay mum for now, okay?"

"Do call him right away. He'll be worried."

As he headed out of the cabin, Keith turned and said, "We'll all be worried."

hiding out

After Keith left, we spent another hour talking about what we were going to do on Friday. I argued that they could get on with their lives and leave me on my boat in its new location, but they felt we should stick together. Logan hated to cancel his classes but decided that's what he was going to do. Judd was less upset than I would have anticipated by the decision to stay away, but then he was going to call in sick and work from home. My only concern was how to let my parents and Sophie know I was okay. We decided that if we got the burner phones early enough, we could call everyone we needed to and spend the rest of the day hiding out on our boats. Hiding out and waiting for calls, from the bad guys and from Keith who was no longer one of the bad guys, or so we hoped.

We all agreed Judd was the one who needed to go purchase the phones since he had never been seen with me. Not that anyone in the area would necessarily recognize any of us, but you never knew for sure. He would use the other folding bike to run his errand. Meanwhile Logan and I would stay behind and hope no one at the marina noticed we were squatting.

Macavity had gone for a stroll shortly after we arrived, and I was hoping he would return soon. I didn't want to be chasing after him if we had to leave on short notice. He wasn't going to like it, but once he came back, his private porthole exit was going to be closed for the duration.

Morning came all too soon. Someone was already calling my name. "Damn," I said as I opened one eye and saw that it was 7:00 a.m.

"Bryn, it's me. Logan." He didn't sound panicked, just persistent.

"I heard you the first time," I yelled back.

"Come over when you can. There's coffee and cinnamon rolls."

Both men liked their creature comforts, and Judd in particular liked regular meals that were both tasty and visually pleasing. I, on the other hand, consider an Eggo gourmet food. Although I have to admit that I've come to appreciate Judd's cooking. Coffee with one of Judd's cinnamon rolls sounded far better than anything I had in my sparse larder, so I dragged myself out of my bunk.

When I saw Macavity staring at his empty bowl I was relived. I quickly went back and closed his exit window before I fed him. Then I headed for the *Carpe Diem.*

"We've already called in sick," Logan said. "Judd found a mini-mart nearby that opened early and picked up some phones. We have the day off." He seemed almost pleased. I had to admit that having a "day off" sounded a lot better than "hiding from the bad guys."

"When was the last time you took a sick day?" I asked. Logan frowned. "I can't remember."

"Me neither," I said as I reached for a mug. Judd was taking the cinnamon rolls out of the oven. They smelled wonderful.

"Oohhh," I said. "What a treat."

"I had them in the freezer," he explained. "It seemed to me

that as long as we're going to be here for a while we might as well indulge ourselves a little."

We drank coffee and had our fill of warm rolls. It almost felt like we were on vacation, although the reality of our situation hung like a thick fog overhead, threatening to descend at any moment.

"I called and left Keith our numbers," Judd said. as we settled back with full stomachs. "He didn't answer, but at least he knows how to get in touch."

"I've been thinking that I will call Sophie and have her call my parents. My mother might get too excited if I try to explain things. Sophie will know how to handle her."

"Will you tell Sophie about Keith?" Logan asked.

"She can't," Judd interjected. "He's an agent and his family sounds like mafia." He turned toward me, "You won't, will you?"

"No, I won't. But it makes it hard to know what to tell her."

"How about something simple like you are making yourself scarce until the bad guys contact you," Logan suggested. "Simple. Basically, the truth. And believable."

Judd nodded.

"She'll ask questions. She knows me."

"Tell her you'll contact her as soon as you know anything. Simple and brief. That's the key."

"Okay," I said, picking up my new phone. "Maybe I'll get lucky and get to leave her a message."

No such luck. Sophie answered on the second ring in spite of not recognizing the number. She didn't even question why I wasn't using my own phone. With Judd and Logan staring at me I was forced to follow their advice. I kept it simple and asked if she would call my parents and tell them. She caught the drift and didn't ask why I would rather she make that call.

"Can do," she said. "And you'll let me know if you hear from the guys who broke into your parents' house." It wasn't a question. "Oh, and have you called Ben?"

"I'll make sure he knows," I said. I didn't want to lie to

Sophie. But since I wasn't entirely sure that Keith would keep his promise to get in touch with Ben, I did intend to follow up and make sure Ben was informed about the latest twist of fate.

It was only 8:00 a.m., and we had done everything on our "to do" lists for the day. Now the hard part was about to begin. Waiting. Waiting and worrying. Hoping the bad guys didn't go to extremes to find us. We weren't invisible, just camouflaged. And we didn't know how long that would last.

Judd was lucky; he had work to do. He got out his computer and spread out a pile of papers. Logan said he had papers to grade but didn't look eager to begin. I suggested a walk down the dock just to stretch our legs.

"Wear hats," Judd ordered without looking up. "And keep that damn cat locked up." I didn't know whether he was concerned about Macavity's safety or just trying to make sure we could make a speedy exit if necessary. Either way, I agreed.

It was nice out, but there was still a touch of morning coolness. I put on a watch cap and tucked my hair inside it. Logan wore a hoody with the hood up. Two redheads in hiding. As we stepped out onto the dock there was no one around. Most of the boats on this particular dock were commercial, with a few pleasure power boats scattered here and there. Our two sailboats stood out more than we had realized the night before with only thin moonlight overhead, but we decided we were sufficiently close to the middle of the long dock that we might get by for a while without being challenged by the marina authorities or spotted by the bad guys.

We wandered past the other boats, stopping from time to time to observe something we found interesting or to comment on some piece of equipment. I had crewed on a salmon troller three summers when I was in college, so I had a warm spot in my heart for the fishing industry, and trollers in particular. Logan was only mildly interested in any boats that didn't sail, but we were both bored, so we spent more time gawking than we might otherwise have done.

When we saw someone at the end of the dock heading in our direction, we slowly turned around and strolled back the way we had come. "Pretend to be a looky-loo," Logan cautioned.

"Is it wise to turn our backs on a stranger at this point?" I asked, feeling more than a little uncomfortable with the situation.

"Hmmm. I didn't think of that." Logan glanced back, his hood not moving with the rest of his head, one eye peering around the edge. "No problem," he said. "He's climbing aboard a boat."

After that we couldn't decide what to do, so we walked to the end of the dock and then headed back to our respective homes. "If someone wonders why we're here," I said, "let's say the *Aspara* had an engine problem and we're waiting for a mechanic to arrive."

"Okay, do you think we'll have to be more specific?"

"If pressed, I can make something up," I assured him. "We'd better tell Judd so we're all on the same page."

Logan decided he would grade some papers, and I returned to the *Aspara* and tried to get my disgruntled cat to use the litter box he hated. There was plenty of work I could have been doing if I'd had access to my files, but I had left my computer in the office, and I had given Keith my cell. I did, however, have plenty of books on board, although I wasn't sure I would be able to relax with a book no matter how good it was. I chose a thriller that promised to be a page turner and stretched out on the settee.

I was obviously not as stressed as I thought because I awoke with a start when someone knocked on the hatch. I sat up and the book I'd been reading slid off onto the floor. Macavity slithered up the stairs, obviously hoping to escape. I picked him up and put him in the bathroom and closed the door. He yowled his displeasure, but unless he knew how to open the door on his own, he wasn't going anywhere.

"Bryn," a male voice said. "It's me, Ben. Let me in."

Ben? If it really was him, maybe Keith was one of the good guys, after all. I unbolted the hatch and pulled it back enough to peek out. Ben was standing there, bending over to let me see his face. "It's me," he repeated. "Can I come aboard?"

"You're supposed to ask permission to come aboard *before* you get on the boat."

"Come on, Bryn, let me in."

I stepped aside and he came down and looked around. I realized he hadn't been on my boat before. "It's not much," I said. "But it's home."

"It's nice. I like the wood."

There was a sound from the bathroom. "Someone here?" he asked.

"Do you mind if I let Macavity out?" I asked.

"No, I like cats."

Macavity burst forth and quickly assessed his chances for escape. Piqued, he jumped up on the settee and checked Ben out. Ben reached over and rubbed his head. Macavity decided a head rub was better than sulking in the other room and plopped himself down alongside Ben.

"I assume this isn't a social call. And . . . how did you know where to find me?" It was the moment of truth.

"Keith McLeod called me."

"And what did he tell you?"

"He filled me in on the situation," he said. "And since it's going to be difficult for him to get back to you, he suggested that I be the link between you and him."

"Did you check him out? Is he who he says he is?"

The corners of Ben's mouth quivered slightly. "And who do you think he is?"

I admitted that I was having to reassess my opinion of Keith. He had helped us get away, but I still had some doubts about who he was working for. "What did he tell *you*?"

"It's nice to know that you can be trusted," Ben said, grinning.

"Don't toy with me. Who do *you* think he works for?"

"Don't worry, I didn't take what he said at face value. He gave me just enough information, so I was able to verify his story. It could be dangerous for him if his connection to the agency gets out, so you really do need to keep it in strict confidence. He's trusting you with his life."

I nodded. Somehow the fact that Keith was risking his life to help me hadn't registered.

"And I assume Judd and Logan are also committed to secrecy."

"Absolutely."

Macavity had his head resting on Ben's leg and was purring contentedly as Ben continued to rub him behind the ears. How did he figure out so quickly what Macavity liked?

"The bad news is that there were no prints on the message and picture left at your parents' house. Several surfaces had been wiped clean. No one saw anything. There are no leads, period. So that looks like a dead-end.

"And by the way, Keith gave me your cell phone. It's being monitored by a colleague. She will let me know when they call."

"Is she going to pretend to be me?"

"Yes. She's trained to handle situations like this."

"But what if they ask her something to test whether it's me. Or what if it's someone I know or I've talked to?"

"We weighed all that when making the decision and decided it's a chance we have to take. All the other options expose your whereabouts. I have her off-site in a secure location. As soon as we hear anything, I'll let you know via your burner. Keith forwarded your burner phone numbers to me."

Keith had certainly been more trusting and open than I'd anticipated. But his own neck was also on the line, so maybe he was doing the smart thing by asking for help.

Ben's phone chose that moment to ring. An anonymous series of atonal notes. It occurred to me that his colleague might be a little surprised when the frogs started in on my cell. That almost made me smile.

After listening and only responding with a few monosyllabic

words, Ben said, "Just a minute," and turned to me. "Get Logan and Judd over here, now."

I left him on the phone and went across to the *Carpe Diem*. When we returned Ben was sitting there tapping his phone on the table. We crammed ourselves into the tiny space as Macavity hastily made a beeline for the forward bunk.

Ben explained to the three of us that whoever left the note at my parents' house had called my cell to make a deal, and that an officer posing as me had handled it. "I'm sorry," he said, looking at me. "She doesn't think she convinced them that you don't have a copy of the research. The story we'd agreed on was that if you'd been in possession of the data in any form you would have turned it over to NorPac. The one thing she thinks they seemed to believe is that you've had a falling out with the 'Say No to Chimeras' group." He shook his head. "They offered money for the research by the way. Quite a bit of money. She felt that by turning it down, they were starting to waver. But then she heard someone in the background say, 'He wouldn't dare lie to us.' Then they hung up."

"Are they going to call back?"

"We don't know. I'll make sure your parents and brother's family have protection while we wait for their next move."

"Do you think the 'he' they referred to is the killer?"

"It seems to me," Judd broke in, "that if the killer didn't get the laptop, then Blaine didn't have it with him."

"And it still bothers me why he was out there in the first place," Logan said. "A non-hiker wearing tennis shoes in the rain."

"It's possible there are two different groups trying for the same thing," Judd said. "In reality things are seldom as simple as they appear on the surface."

"It could even be someone looking for revenge," I said. The sentiment was a showstopper. Everyone stared at me.

"What do you mean?" Ben asked.

"Well, I keep thinking about the family that Blaine refused to help. Not that he could have done what they were asking. But they were going through a tough time and not acting rationally. Maybe his rejection has been festering. Maybe they finally decided to get even." I paused to consider whether I believed what I was saying or not. "Not that it makes any sense. Given the timing and all. But they thought he was their last hope, and he refused. And their daughter died. It wasn't cause-and-effect, but they might see it that way."

"I'll look into it," Ben said as he jotted a note in a pocket-sized spiral pad.

"And what about Blaine's parents? Do we assume they're being squeezed by the same people?" Logan asked.

"We have a trace on their phone, but no one has gotten back to them."

"I feel so sorry for them," I said. "I keep thinking that someone needs to tell them the truth."

As if on cue, Ben's phone rang again. He listened without saying much, then signed off. "Well, you won't have to wait long for them to know the truth. They just found Jared Blaine's body."

Those were words I'd been expecting. Yet at the back of my mind, I had clung to the tiny hope that maybe I'd been wrong, that maybe he hadn't been dead and had walked away from the scene of the accident in spite of a broken leg. Although deep down, I knew he had died in that ravine.

"Your friend in Scotland called to tell you and was surprised to find that someone else was answering your phone." Ben stood up. "Well, I have a number of things to follow up on."

"What do *we* do now?" I asked.

Ben gave me an indulgent smile and turned to Judd. "You want to tell her?" For some reason of late everyone seemed to consider Judd the pragmatic, cool-headed one. Logan and I were the wild cards.

"I'll get back to you as soon as I know something." Ben climbed up the stairs and disappeared. "We wait," Judd said.

The rest of Friday was boring beyond belief. Judd and Logan kept themselves busy with work related tasks. I started several books, including a second guaranteed page turner that the critics promised you couldn't put down. They were wrong.

Macavity moped about and napped on the forward bunk, occasionally demanding treats which I gave him out of guilt for keeping him locked up. I would have to put him on a diet after this was over.

Judd fixed a wonderful dinner from odds and ends he had aboard. He limited us each to one glass of wine with dinner in case we needed to make a clear-headed and quick departure. We only heard a few people come down the dock, and no one paid any undue attention to our presence there. The weekend might bring more activity on the docks, but we were all hoping for a reprieve by then. Unfortunately, our burner cells remained silent.

The boring day turned into a boring evening. I kept telling myself that boring was better than being threatened. But I wasn't sure how many days of waiting around for something to happen I could stand.

For once Macavity and I were in agreement.

CHAPTER 26

night visitor

There was a light "rap, rap, rap" on my hatch. I rolled over and looked at the clock: 2:04 a.m. Macavity rolled over too but continued to sleep. It was much too early for him to care about guests, or potential threats.

I made my way into the galley and said, "Who's there?"

"Keith." He said his name just loud enough for me to hear it.

With only a moment's hesitation, I slid the hatch open. "Sorry to wake you up," he said in that lovely brogue. I started to ask how he knew I'd been asleep then realized I was wearing a rather skimpy nightgown.

"Just a sec," I said and went to get a robe. I was almost sorry my robe was a ratty old thing that I'd had for ages. Not something to entertain a handsome guest in. But then, I reminded myself sternly, just because he wasn't a bad guy didn't mean a relationship with him was a possibility. He had, after all, been doing his job by approaching me in the first place.

When I returned, he was seated and leaning back against the settee cushions just like he belonged there. Con man or not, he certainly had some high voltage masculine appeal. "You talked to Ben," I said when he didn't say anything.

"You looked better before," he commented with an impish grin.

I tugged my robe closer and tried not to feel flattered. He'd had his chance in Scotland. "So, do we need to wake Logan and Judd, or do you have some information for my ears only?" The tone I was trying for was jaunty yet business-like; but I don't think I achieved the effect. Damn. He really threw me off my stride.

"No need to wake them. I just wanted to make sure everything was okay and clarify a few things. I want to avoid using phones unless absolutely necessary." He smiled again. "And it's nicer to talk in person."

"Would you like a cup of tea?" I asked as I put the kettle on to make myself one.

"Yes, please. With milk and sugar if you have it."

I got out the mugs and opened my refrigerator to make certain I had milk. I always keep some canned milk on board in case I run out of the real thing, but I still had enough to indulge his cultural preference. "Decaf?" I asked as I went through what I had in my tea drawer.

"That isn't tea," he said.

I got out the strongest black tea I had and plopped a bag in his mug. After wavering between a black decaf or a green tea, I chose the green. Although I can handle a lot of caffeine and still sleep, there was something about the hour and situation that called for a soothing drink.

"Mind if we start at the beginning?" he asked after doctoring his tea and taking the first sip.

"Which beginning?"

"From when you found the body. And this time don't leave anything out."

I walked him through what had happened, admitting how spooked I'd felt even though I didn't have any real evidence that someone was watching from the trees. He took a few notes as I told him who I'd talked to after I'd discovered the body, prompting me to try and remember what I'd said to them and what they had said to me. Finally, he asked if I'd made any attempt to investigate Blaine's whereabouts on my own, and I realized, if I was to be totally honest, I'd have to confess about searching Jared's room at the inn. He seemed surprised, but not judgmental. Given his line of work, what I had done was probably standard procedure.

"Someone had already gone through his things and removed his identification," he summarized. "Odd."

"That's what it looked like. And after that there were the two calls to the inn saying he was extending his trip and would eventually be back to pick up his things. They apparently even sent money to cover the cost of the room."

"Whoever did that had to know it wasn't going to work for long."

"Maybe they were hoping to make it more difficult to pinpoint the time of death," I said.

"It sounds like a panic move to me. Or, they may have been stalling for time."

"Time to locate the research data, you mean."

"Yes. But if the killer was the first one to search the room, why didn't he find the laptop or whatever device the data was stored on?" Keith seemed truly puzzled.

"We don't know that he didn't."

"Actually, the people who have been hassling you have asked me to look into the possibility that someone beat the killer to the information. Someone other than you."

"How convenient."

"Yes, occasionally things work out. Anyway, I'm flying back to Scotland tomorrow morning." He looked at his watch. "Correction—*this* morning."

"Where do you start?"

"By talking to everyone who knew Blaine was there. And everyone you talked to about finding the body."

"Short list."

"Very short."

"Well, it couldn't have been one of the rescue people. They didn't believe I actually found a body."

"But we don't know who they talked to. I need to follow the trail, wherever it leads. It's even possible someone took the data *before* Blaine was killed. The only thing we know for sure is that it had to be someone who knew Blaine was in the area and who knew or guessed that he had the data with him."

Keith finished off his tea and looked ready to leave.

"Will you be in touch?" I asked. "In case I think of something."

Keith hesitated. "Is there something you aren't telling me?"

"I've told you everything I know," I said truthfully. The other ideas that were percolating at the back of my mind were wild speculation.

"Well, the good news is that you should be able to get back to normal soon. At least for now. I'll let you know if they change their minds and intend to come after you again."

"What did they think when we disappeared into the night?"

"That you were frightened. So, you might want to wait a day or so before returning to the marina. I wouldn't want them to connect your reappearance to me."

Great, I had another boring day ahead of me.

When he stood up, I got up too. Suddenly I became very conscious of his proximity in the small space. And for some reason I wasn't surprised when he stepped over and kissed me on the mouth. "Take care of yourself, Bryn."

He certainly knew how to make an exit. And he was a great kisser.

Macavity let me sleep until 9:30. Then he couldn't stand it any longer. He demanded breakfast. I got up and filled his bowl before making coffee. Next, I took a quick shower, using as little water as possible; I was running low on water. But I could make it another day . . . or two, if necessary. Monday morning at the latest, I told myself. That was my deadline for getting back to normal.

Logan and Judd had apparently been up for hours by the time I went over to the *Carpe Diem*. Both were hard at work, although Logan asked if I was up for a short walk. He was getting antsy. First, I told them about my visit from Keith and what he had said. "I wonder if he's informed Ben?" Judd asked.

"I should have asked him, but I didn't think of it," I admitted.

"Well, at least it sounds as though we can relax a little."

"We should probably wait until Ben contacts us before we head back to the marina," Judd cautioned.

"Hopefully we can go back by Monday."

Both men agreed. It felt like I was up for parole, waiting for a panel to decide my fate.

Playing it safe, I decided to keep Macavity inside another day. Or at least until we'd heard from Ben. Logan and I did our hat and hoody routine again for our walk. But we felt much more at ease.

"I wonder how long we could stay tied up here for free?" Logan asked.

"Oh, I'm sure if we were on a transient dock, they'd be all over us to pay up. As long as the real tenants don't show up, we are probably okay."

"Well, I expect someone official to come by today with a bill for moorage," Logan said. "They may even ask us to move." We took several more short walks during the day. There were two different dock locations at the marina. The original wood docks were lined up along a cement bulkhead with finger floats in various stages of disrepair. These were used by a combination of pleasure and commercial boats. Shops, a café and a restaurant formed a barrier between the marina and the street. Another area had been renovated for larger commercial boats. You could get to it by walking to the other end of the marina past designated work areas for repairing nets and storing pots and a brick building that had restrooms and showers.

Walking past the working boats brought back those summers I'd spent on a troller. It had been hard work, but I had savored the moments of calm evenings in harbor, fishing alongside majestic humpbacks, the early morning thrill of first catch, the shimmering rainbow scales of a king salmon coming out of the water, the way the water and sky would sometimes blend together in a single metallic silver backdrop. One downside had been the unpleasant aroma of fish guts and blood that hovered over the cockpit. No matter how much you scrubbed, unpleasant fishy odors lingered. After being out on the boat for a while, however, the fishy smell became less obnoxious and merged into the overall experience and the many happy hours spent on the water.

Other than a few leisurely walks, the three of us stayed on our respective boats. Macavity got more and more agitated by his enforced imprisonment. And I got more and more cranky waiting for news of what was happening. And then I got careless.

I pulled back the hatch to go over to the *Carpe Diem*, and Macavity rushed past me, an orange streak of lightening. I called out for him to come back, but no self-respecting cat lets his owner interfere with something he really wants to do. And Macavity really wanted to stretch his legs and explore his new surroundings.

I went over and told Logan and Judd what had happened and said I was going to go after him. They said I should wait; he would come back when he felt like it, and we probably weren't leaving any time soon anyway. But I couldn't just wait. I was worried. And to be honest, looking for Macavity sounded a lot more interesting than trying to read a novel I wasn't into.

It isn't easy to think like a cat. And even a large orange cat can stay hidden when he wants to. After searching and calling his name up and down the docks, I gave up and returned to the *Aspara*. Logan and Judd came out to see whether I'd been successful. "No cat?" Judd asked. I shook my head.

"Just leave his window open," Logan advised. "He'll get hungry and come home."

"Speaking of food . . . " Judd said dinner was almost ready. Apparently, as long as we were on the run he was going to make dinner for the three of us. In spite of my concern about Macavity I felt my taste buds tingle. He really was an excellent cook.

After dinner Logan and I took one last look around for Macavity before calling it a night. We scared a couple of seagulls off the dock, but we didn't find my irritating and irreplaceable cat. Logan kept assuring me that cats like to wander, and he reminded me that no matter how smart and special he was, Macavity was at heart a cat.

I read for a while, then went to my bunk and tried to sleep. My mind refused to cooperate. First, I would picture all of the horrible things that could happen to Macavity. Ravenous dogs. Crazed fishermen. Falling into the water. On and on.

Then my thoughts would go back to that day in Scotland, and I would relive finding Blaine's body. At this point there was no doubt that Blaine had died somewhere on that trail or at the bottom of the ravine. But the puzzle remained as to why he was out there in the first place. And I kept coming back to the guilt I felt for not sticking around and calling for help right away. It wouldn't have saved his life, but it would have saved a lot of the grief that followed.

The last time I remembered looking at the clock it said 3:15 a.m.

When I woke up, the sun was shining through the porthole. I have insets that I put in them for privacy when tied to a dock, but I'd forgotten to put them in the night before. And I was glad I had. Because the sun was shining directly on the orange body I have come to adore.

I slipped out of bed and quickly closed his porthole exit. Gotcha, Macavity, I said to myself. I hope your night on the town was worth it. Because you're in for the duration now.

home sweet home

Sunday was the longest day in recent history. At least for me. No internet. No computer. No files to work on. No Macavity to chase down. Just endless hours to speculate about whether there was a simple answer that would explain who had killed Blaine and who had made off with his data.

If Keith was right that the organization he was working for hadn't killed Blaine but were taking advantage of his death to get their hands on the data, then someone else was responsible for Blaine's death as well as for the missing research materials. There was also the question of who was responsible for beating up Conrad. Although it seemed unlikely, I hadn't entirely eliminated Keith's dubious connections from that despicable act. As soon as I got a reprieve from my self-imposed exile, I wanted to talk with Conrad about what he had found out before someone tried to shut him up.

The "Say No" group—or some rogue members of the group —were still high on my list of suspects, for both Blaine's murder and for having stolen his data. After all, one of them had likely taken a shot at me. Perhaps he or she had been acting alone, but they were a passionate, tight-knit group. It was entirely possible that they had managed to get their hands on Blaine's computer and were waiting for the right moment to make a dramatic announcement about the horrors of his research. Of course, if they admitted to having the data, that would also suggest they may have had a hand in Blaine's death.

Perhaps that was why they hadn't said anything yet.

Nor was I completely ruling out MedTech as a devil corporation, masking its evil intent behind apparent transparency. There might even be another competitor out there spooking around, hoping to get their hands on the potentially profitable information from Blaine's scientific research. A person or group that wasn't even on our radar yet but had either been involved in Blaine's murder or the race to recover his information and claim it as their own.

For a time, I even considered the possibility that Bill had stolen his colleague's data and was going to wait until he could establish his path to fame by slowly integrating what Blaine had accomplished into his own work. But somehow, I had a hard time picturing Bill as the villain of the piece. He had been too honest about not knowing much about Blaine's project. And he would have needed help, because there was no evidence that he had left the country. Although, again, he could have simply taken advantage of the situation and confiscated Blaine's computer once he went missing. We had only his word for the fact that Blaine had taken all his devices with him.

Since none of my flights of fancy produced any solid answers, I decided that maybe we weren't asking the right questions. Maybe Blaine hadn't been killed because of his research. What if it had been a more personal reason? My thoughts kept coming back to the couple whose daughter had died. Surely after her death they realized that neither the doctor nor Blaine had any real choice in the matter. It was just unfortunate that Blaine hadn't handled the situation better. And that the doctor and hospital hadn't been sufficiently sympathetic when explaining the facts of the situation. But under the circumstances, why kill the researcher and not the doctor?

The other possibility that threw a wrench into all my other theories was the possibility that Blaine had been killed by a complete stranger. I hadn't seen other hikers, but maybe he had run into someone who had tried to rob him, and he had fought back and fallen into the ravine by accident. Or, maybe he had been robbed first and pushed over the edge with his backpack. They could have taken his electronics without realizing the significance of what they were stealing.

The more I thought about it, however, the more likely it seemed to me that someone had taken the laptop and tablet from Blaine's room at the inn.

Unfortunately, none of those scenarios explained why Blaine's body had been moved. Nor did they explain the attempts to delay discovery of his death. And why was he on the trail in the first place? Why? There were too many whys.

As my mind struggled with the myriad of possible scenarios, I started wondering whether the doctor who'd had the responsibility for telling the Davidsons that their daughter didn't qualify for a transplant had been hounded by them since. That could indicate whether they had moved on or not. It might be worthwhile to talk to him about the incident and what had happened since then, if anything. It might also be interesting to ask him whether he and Blaine had talked about the Davidsons' proposal.

When Logan stopped by to see how I was doing, I suggested this to him, and he balked.

"Bryn, haven't these people suffered enough?"

"But what if they're still angry? What if their loss has driven them to finally seek revenge?"

"What if they have been trying to rebuild their lives, to adjust to their loss? Do you want to bring it all up again?"

"They won't know if I talk to the doctor," I argued.

"I think you should let it go. Let Ben and Keith and the Scottish police do their jobs."

Perhaps I was overthinking everything in the absence of being able to do anything but think. Once we were able to go home and

I returned to my routine, maybe then I would be able to step away.

Ben came by at dinnertime, and Judd offered him some stew. Ben started to decline, then took a deep breath of the incredible mixture of flavors filling the cabin and changed his mind. Stew to Judd was a work of art. The searing, the spices, the layering of root vegetables, the right wine in the pot and with the meal. As much as I wanted to hear Ben say we could go home, there was at least one part of being on the run that I would miss.

After we'd had our fill, Ben announced that it was probably safe to return to the marina. His conclusion was mostly based on what Keith had told him; there had been no progress made on discovering who had made the threats to my parents and no leads as to who had killed Blaine. Still, it was nice to have my phone back, and I was looking forward to having access to my computer. Being totally offline had been unsettling. I hadn't realized how dependent on technology I'd become.

"In fact," Ben said, "there is no real evidence that it was murder. Although it looks like he had been in a fight. Based on the physical evidence, it's equally possible that he fell by accident or that someone pushed him over the edge."

"I can't imagine that he would have rolled all the way down that hill from the trail and hit his head on the boulder," I said.

"Maybe the fight didn't start at the top of the hill," Ben suggested. "We may never know."

"Unless we find the killer," I said.

"Unless the Scottish police find the assailant," Ben corrected.

I nodded. It was one thing to let the authorities do their job if they were making progress, another if they weren't getting anywhere.

We took our time after dinner, enjoying our coffee and then a glass of wine. In some ways we were reluctant to end our time away. It had been stressful and relaxing at the same time.

Macavity was the only one anxious to get going. I couldn't blame him for wanting his freedom back.

It didn't take long before we were back at our marina home. Logan helped adjust the fenders for rafting up to the *Carpe Diem*. We had agreed that I would spend another day or two alongside the *Carpe Diem* before going back to my own slip. Just as a precautionary measure.

Minutes after I turned the engine off, Macavity leapt out of the open hatch and raced like a deranged critter across the *Carpe Diem* to the dock. He paused briefly when he realized where he was, then he slowed down and sauntered off. He was home. Or close enough.

a visit to the doctor

First thing Monday morning I strolled down the familiar dock to my office. The sun was out, boats bounced ever so slightly in their slips from the wake of a boat passing by, and a murder of crows were raising a ruckus next to the lockers. The usual sights and sounds of marina life. How I loved the place, especially during the day, and now that I probably didn't have to worry about someone lurking in the shadows at night.

After unlocking the two locks on my office door, I stepped inside. Everything looked normal. Normal, that is, for a cluttered mess of a workplace. Bubbles IV was still alive, thank heavens. Did he look thinner? I couldn't tell. But my first official act was to feed him or her. I'd always felt like his predecessors were female, but for some reason this one seemed more masculine. Not that he looked any different from the others. But there was something about the way he moved. More of a swagger than a mermaid waggle.

The second thing I did was call Sophie at work. She answered right away. "It's about time."

"It's only been three days," I pointed out.

"Seemed longer."

"How is Conrad?" I asked, changing the subject.

"He's doing fine. He's out of the hospital. Staying with a

friend until he feels well enough to return to work. Maybe by the end of the week."

"That's good news."

"Yes."

"Have you talked with him more about what preceded the beating? Who he talked to, that kind of thing?"

"Yes, he asked a few members if they knew anything about the shooting, but he didn't get anywhere with that. Nor did he come across anyone who was particularly concerned about whether you might have Blaine's research. He said everyone just seemed happy that Blaine was no longer around. If he stepped on anyone's toes by asking questions, he wasn't aware of it."

"Unless some of the people he talked to kept silent because they think he and I were in cahoots."

"'Cahoots'? Nobody says 'cahoots,' Bryn."

"What should I have said?"

"A simple 'working together' would do. Maybe 'collaborating.' Or 'conspiring together.' Something like that."

"So, what if they think Conrad and I are 'conspiring together'?"

"He admits there is a fringe element in the group. Maybe even a few people who would be more motivated by money than principle. But he's reluctant to believe that someone in the group attacked him."

"Okay. But just so you know, I'm not ruling out that possibility."

"I doubt the police are either."

We were interrupted by someone stopping by Sophie's office to talk to her. She said she had to run and we could continue our conversation later. I hadn't had a chance to ask her how my parents had responded when she told them I would be out of touch for a while. I decided not to find out for myself and put off making the call to them.

As pleased as I was to be back, I couldn't help feeling a lack of closure. It was like reading three-quarters of a book you were really into and then just stopping. I leaned back in my chair and watched Bubbles IV circling for a while. That's how I felt, like I was running in circles, thinking in circles, and circled by people with different agendas. And I could either keep spinning and wait for others with a less personal interest in the case to figure things out. Or not.

Okay, I would leave the heavy lifting to the officials on the case. There were, however, a few loose ends I felt I could tie up without stepping on any toes or endangering myself or my family. Lines of investigation no one else would bother to pursue. Stray thoughts that continued to niggle. If I was ever going to move on, I needed to rid myself of those niggles.

Both Logan and Judd had gone back to work today, so I was on my own. With the help of my trusty computer search engine, it didn't take me long to locate Dr. Robbie Robinson at a nearby specialty clinic. Although I had never tried to get five minutes of a doctor's time before just to talk with him about a nonmedical related issue, I soon discovered that scheduling five minutes with this particular doctor, whether today or a year from today, wasn't going to happen. Especially since I said it was a private matter. I couldn't even get past his first line of defense. Undaunted, I decided I would go hang out at the clinic for a while to see what was possible in person.

His name on the reader board at the entrance to the clinic was listed as "Dr. Robbie Robinson, M.D." Was "Robbie" a play on his last name? Or had his parents really named him Rob or Robert Robinson? Either way, I've never been fond of men's nicknames that end in "ie." It's always seemed to me they should give up the "ie" as a rite of passage into manhood. Not that I'm opinionated about such things.

There were three schedulers at the entrance. One was a stern looking woman with an old-fashioned hairdo and a navy-blue blouse covered with disproportionately large and colorful flowers. The second was a young man with an earnest expression and slightly harried demeanor. I decided on cubicle number three and a middle-aged man with a scant wave of hair over a balding spot on the top of his head. I wasn't wild about the hair, but he looked calm and pleasant.

"Do you have an appointment?" he asked as I stopped in front of the narrow desk that separated the ailing from the workers.

I explained that my doctor had referred me to Dr. Robinson, and I just wanted to get a glimpse of him, get a feel for what he was like, maybe ask him a couple of questions before making the appointment. "You can see a picture of him on our website," he said.

"That isn't the same," I said. "And I'm nervous about this. Probably being silly. But this is a big deal to me."

He seemed to be considering my request. I waited patiently while he made up his mind, afraid to say anything that would tip the scales against me. Finally, he referred me to the third floor and said he would call one of the attendants up there and see if they could accommodate me. "Not that I'm promising it *will* happen," he emphasized. "But I do understand."

I was about to head for the elevator when he stopped me to ask for my name. There was no reason why I couldn't have told him the truth, but for some reason I didn't. "Chrissy," I said, "Chrissy Christianson." Chrissy meets Robbie. It could be the title of a very bad movie.

The person who asked for my name when I reached the third floor did not seem as receptive to the idea of letting me check out Dr. Robinson, but she didn't say "no" either. I explained I would just like to see him, and, if he had a few moments, ask him about his philosophy of medicine as a profession. "Really?" she asked. "You can see that on our website. Along with his education, where he's practiced, as well as his outside interests and hobbies. It's all there." She sounded like she didn't approve of so much information being available to the public.

"I just want to get a feel for what he's like," I said, trying to sound reasonable. "This is a referral. I usually go to female physicians, and I'm uncomfortable seeing a male doctor. You do understand, don't you?"

She hesitated. "He's a very busy man," she said. I could tell by her tone that she was wavering. I did my best to look sympathetic and needy. She stared me down for what felt like an eternity before relenting. "All right, I'll pass along your request and see what he says. Please take a seat."

I took a seat as directed and thumbed through a two-month-old People Magazine. Did patients steal the newer ones, or did someone bring in their old magazines after they'd read them? I've always wondered about that. Once I'd ripped out a recipe from a waiting room magazine, feeling incredibly guilty. It was only afterwards that I wondered if there'd been a camera in the room. When they hadn't included the cost of the magazine in my bill, I was relieved.

About fifteen minutes later a man in a white coat emerged from a hallway and looked in my direction. He was better looking in person than in his website picture. Early forties, sculpted features, curly brown hair. And tall. For a moment I regretted being Chrissy.

"Chrissy?" he asked as he approached and extended his hand.

I stood up and firmly grasped his hand. "Thank you for taking a few minutes to see me," I said.

"Patty said you wanted to meet me before setting up an appointment. Are there any questions I can answer for you?"

You could have knocked me over. If I ever did have a medical issue that required his expertise I would definitely sign up. But his warm demeanor and big brown eyes made me feel so guilty I could barely speak.

"I'm sorry," I said. "I want to ask you about something that happened a few years ago. I'm not a potential patient."

He looked more puzzled than angry. "Are you here on behalf of someone else?"

"No, I'm here because . . . I've become a target for a group called 'Say No to Chimeras,' and I thought if I could ask you a few questions about your experience with the Davidsons it might be helpful."

I had to give him credit; he didn't miss a beat. "Well, Chrissy, if you want to talk to me over lunch, that would be fine. I usually eat in the cafeteria around 11:30."

"Thank you so much," I said. "I'll be there."

He surprised me again by smiling before turning and heading back down the aisle. I caught a glimpse of Patty standing nearby. She'd probably overheard our conversation and *she* definitely wasn't smiling. I hurried past her with a brief nod of thanks.

Even though the scheduler at the desk might eventually get an earful from Patty or the doctor about my subterfuge, I stopped to thank him. "Dr. Robinson seems great," I said truthfully. I could have added: And handsome. And charming. And I was going to have lunch with him. Well, not exactly a date, but I did wonder if he was single. I couldn't help having noticed his lack of a wedding ring, although maybe he took it off at work because of all the handwashing. Or to avoid being labeled as married. I am so suspicious.

With a couple of hours to kill I walked around the hospital complex, checked out the cafeteria, and stumbled across a Starbucks. A cup of coffee is always a welcome diversion. But as I was sipping the aromatic brew it crossed my mind that McDreamy might not be what he seemed. Maybe at lunchtime I would find myself sitting across from a security cop in the cafeteria. Or, even if he intended to meet me, he could have a medical emergency and end up a no-show. What would I do then? Damn. I should have used my real name.

I was hungry, so I decided to go through the cafeteria line early and pick up something to eat while waiting. I got a bowl of clam chowder and a muffin and found a table off to the side with a view of the entrance to the area. I didn't have long to wait before he came through carrying his tray.

He looked around, saw me, smiled, and headed over. There wasn't a security guard in sight.

"I don't have long, Chrissy," he said as he took his lunch off his tray and set the tray aside. Then he sat down and picked up his sandwich.

"Well, the first thing you need to know is that my name is Bryn Baczek. And I'm so sorry I lied."

He had his sandwich all the way to his mouth but paused to look at me instead of taking a bite. "Bryn," he repeated. "That's a nice name."

"I didn't think they'd let me in to talk to you," I said in way of explanation. "Although I'm not sure what that has to do with using a phony name."

He didn't seem phased by the admission. "Tell me about the 'Say No' people. What's going on there?"

I gave him a quick overview, explaining that I'd discovered a body when hiking in Scotland, that it had turned out to be a local researcher, and that I'd gone to a 'Say No to Chimeras' meeting to learn more about the controversy. Skipping over a few details, I told him that someone got it into their heads that I was a spy. And things had gone downhill from there.

"What does this have to do with the Davidsons?"

"The police think that a NorPac rival, or maybe a 'Say No' group member, may be responsible for Blaine's death. And that seems likely. But I read that article in the newspaper about the Davidsons, and it made me wonder if they or someone related to them could be involved. If not in his death, then in trying to get their hands on the research. I know it's a longshot, but I'm hoping you may be able to share some insight into their state of mind at the time, whatever isn't covered by confidentiality, that is. I'm also wondering whether they've been in contact with you more recently."

He put what remained of his sandwich back on the plate. "It was a terrible situation," he said. "They refused to accept the committee's decision. That's why it got into the news. The hospital felt forced into making a statement. And although I felt for the family, I agreed that she wasn't a good candidate for the transplant. There are so many requests—you have to make tough choices. Unfortunately, Mrs. Davidson was very emotional. And vocal. Mr. Davidson wasn't much better, but he was more in control on the surface.

"The only one who didn't want to talk to the press was Melissa's brother. So of course, they kept trying to corner him, asking really inflammatory questions. But he was too overwhelmed to say much of anything."

"He was pretty young at the time, wasn't he?"

"Yes, I can't remember his name. I felt so sorry for him. He was losing his sister, and his parents were both having meltdowns. Anyway, that time at the hospital when there was the, ah, exchange that got all the press coverage was the last time I saw them. Or heard from them."

He returned to his sandwich and I managed to get a few spoons of soup to my mouth without dribbling it down my chin. Soup is not a good thing to eat in company. A person sipping and dribbling is not a pretty sight. Although almost any food can be disastrous when you're trying to make an impression. And I was apparently trying, at least a bit.

"Have *you* talked with them?" he asked.

I put my spoon down. "No, I don't have any official role in the investigation. And it seems a bit awkward to bring up their daughter in connection with what I'm going through."

He glanced at his watch. "I hate to cut this short. Maybe we could continue our conversation over drinks?"

"Ah," I began, pleased and surprised at the same time.

He glanced at my left hand. "I don't see a ring, but I understand if you would rather not."

I didn't have to take long to decide. "I'm not married. And I would enjoy talking with you over drinks." I assumed that meant he wasn't married either, but I was reluctant to ask.

He took out a card, handed it to me and suggested a time and place that I agreed to. "Oh, by the way," he said as he stood up to take his leave. "That's my real name."

I quickly reached into my purse and retrieved a card. "And this is mine."

"You didn't look like a Chrissy," he said as he picked up his tray and left me sitting there with a half-eaten muffin and the cold remains of my chowder.

Back at the office I used Pipl to find the name of the Davidsons' son: Quentin. From there it was a piece of cake to learn more about him. He was an active Facebook user, and it didn't take much effort to find photos he had posted of himself and two friends. They looked like average young men having a good time.

The problem was that they were having a good time in Scotland.

an almost date?

Logan stopped by my office to let me know he was back from the university, and probably to make sure I was okay. I quickly motioned him in. Then I pulled up Quentin's Facebook page with the Scotland photos and turned my laptop around for Logan to see.

"Do you know who this is?"

"Which one?"

There were of at least three and sometimes more young guys in each of the pictures. "This one," I said, pointing out Quentin. "His name is Quentin. Notice where they are?"

Logan studied the pictures. "Scotland?"

"Yes, Scotland. And Quentin's last name is Davidson. Ring any bells?"

Logan blinked a couple of times, then looked more closely at the pictures. "You don't mean . . ."

"Yes, that's exactly what I mean."

"But you don't think he . . ."

"That's exactly what I think."

He leaned back. "Are you going to tell Ben?" he asked.

"I would like to talk to Quentin first. It's possible this is just a coincidence."

"But you don't believe that."

"I'm not sure. I mean, he's with a group of kids. And the pictures are on Facebook. If he was stalking Blaine, it wasn't a very subtle plan."

"So, what are you going to do?"

"I have a phone number for him, and I'm thinking about giving him a call and setting up a meeting. Maybe at a coffee shop. Would you be willing to go with me?"

"Sure. But I still think handing this off to Ben is a better idea. Even if the kid did it, he's not going to confess."

"I guess I just want to get a sense of what he's like. He and his family have gone through so much. And once I turn his name over to Ben, the police are going to assume he's involved."

"You think your gut will tell you whether he's a killer or not?"

"You disapprove?"

Logan thought about the question for a minute. "Not really. I'm just not sure how productive meeting with him will be." He paused briefly. "Oh, what the hell, count me in."

"Good, I'll call him first thing tomorrow. Meanwhile, I'll walk you down the dock. I need to change."

"Where are you going?"

"I have a kinda date."

"Really?"

"Don't look so surprised."

"I just can't imagine how you managed to find time to meet someone to go out with, even for a 'kinda' date. Unless it's Ben—is it?"

"No, not Ben." Then I explained that I had gone to see the doctor who had turned down the Davidsons and that he had asked me out for drinks.

"You really know how to turn an investigation into an opportunity," Logan kidded as we headed down the dock. "But I'm not sure you should be driving back alone later." Then he grinned. "I assume you'll be coming back on your own."

"It's not even a real date," I said. "Just a continuation of our conversation at the hospital."

"Whatever it is, you'll call me when you're on your way, okay? If you're alone, I'll walk you back to the *Aspara*."

I thought he was overreacting; we were supposed to be back to normal. But on the other hand, it didn't hurt to be cautious, so I agreed.

Deciding what to wear was problematic. If I overdid it, Robbie would think I was making a play for him. If I didn't clean up a little, he would think I wasn't interested. A balancing act. I settled for black slacks and a comfortable tunic that said, "arty but casual." Fortunately, it didn't need ironing because I was cutting it close to get there on time.

Robbie was just walking toward the entrance when I arrived. He stopped when he saw me pull into the parking lot. "It's good to see you," he said as I joined him.

"It's good to see you too," I said with my inimitable cleverness.

Once inside things got easier. We ordered wine and hors d oeuvres and chatted about his practice, my profession, the weather. Then we discovered our mutual interest in sailing. He told me he had a 49' ketch moored in front of his parents' home on the lake. He explained that his father liked to take it out occasionally, and so did his brother. Unfortunately, he didn't have as much time to go sailing as he would like, so he was pleased that his family used it. And, his dad did some of the upkeep, so that was a plus too.

"My daughter wanted to name our boat the Blood Vessel, but I overruled her," he added.

"You have a daughter?" I felt a flutter of disappointment.

"Yes, she's fourteen. Not an easy age." To my questioning look he said, "Divorced. Four years ago, when Roberta was ten."

Roberta? "You don't call her Robbie, Jr., do you?" I *had* to ask.

He laughed. "No, we used to call her Robo—long story. But she demands that we call her by her full name now."

"Do you have custody?"

"Joint. And it's working out okay."

"So, what is the boat's name?" I asked, wanting to get off the subject of divorce.

"*Roberta*," he said. "It was the only way we could get her to give up on *Blood Vessel*."

Once the preliminaries were over with, we talked briefly about the Davidsons. Quentin had been a silent figure in the background to Robbie; he had nothing much to say about him. When I asked about Melissa, he described her as a sweet and appealing young girl. He added that he couldn't imagine what he would have done if the decision to deny a needed transplant had been made about his own daughter. That's why it had been easy for him to overlook the fuss the Davidsons had made. And, although he said he had never talked with Blaine about the situation, he knew about what the Davidsons had asked of him.

"Of course, I could never have agreed to participate even if I'd wanted to. It would have been illegal."

The rest of the evening was uneventful. We ordered several more hors d oeuvres and decided we were too full to eat an actual dinner. But he asked me if I would like to have dinner with him another time, and I said "yes." He was comfortable and pleasant, but there were no sparks between us, at least none that I discerned. Still, I had no doubt that my mother would label him a real catch.

When he walked me to my car he asked if I was okay going home alone. It didn't sound like a come-on, so I assured him I was. I didn't add that there would be someone meeting me at the parking lot. I hadn't told him about the recent threats. Or how we had gone into hiding. Or that someone had skewered my goldfish. The events of the last month seemed so bizarre, and I felt like that was maybe too much detail at this point in what might have the potential to become a relationship.

I called Logan when I was just a few minutes out and both he and Judd met me at the parking lot to walk me back. It was a lovely evening, mild and still. A full moon stared down at us, a round golden orb of light. The boats moved slowly and almost silently in their slips. The marina was still full of shadows and dark corners, but they no longer seemed like hiding places for potential assailants. It was starting to feel like home again.

"So, how was Dr. Robinson?" Logan asked.

"Very nice."

"Oh, oh. That sounds like an 'almost' date."

"I did agree to see him again."

"Ouch," Logan said. "You 'agreed' to 'see him again.' My prediction—this isn't going anywhere."

I didn't comment. It did cross my mind that none of my relationships the past few years had gone anywhere. It was becoming a pattern. If I didn't watch out, I would end up as an independent woman on her own. Maybe with a lover or two on the side. Not a bad way to live, come to think of it.

CHAPTER 30

“ ’

i'm not stupid

”

Monday morning Fiona called to see if everything was okay. She'd heard that Keith was back in the area and asking questions about Blaine's death. She couldn't figure out what he was up to and asked if I had any thoughts on it. I was sorry I couldn't tell her that Keith wasn't really a con man or a criminal. But my lips were sealed as tight as a lid on a Mason jar.

"Still no leads?" I asked.

None that she knew of. If something didn't pop soon, they would probably put Blaine's death in the unsolved column.

After hanging up I called Quentin. I had tried to come up with a reasonable explanation for why I wanted to talk to him without giving away the fact that I knew he had been in Scotland when Blaine went missing. Our only other link was Blaine's research. So, when he answered his phone, I explained that I had an interest in better understanding the potential for what was referred to as "chimera research" and had considered talking to his parents but thought it might be too painful for them. Would he be willing to talk to me about what they had learned?

He immediately wanted to know where I got his name, and I said that I knew Dr. Robinson. I didn't mention that I had only known him for a day.

214

Quentin didn't say anything for a few seconds, and I wondered if he was going to hang up on me. But he didn't. "Sure," he said finally without asking any more questions. "How about three o'clock?" He named a coffee shop near where he lived for our rendezvous. After I hung up, I realized that I hadn't mentioned that I was bringing Logan with me. Would that turn him off? Maybe I'd have Logan wait in the car initially and come in as if he just happened to be in the neighborhood. Since he worked at the university it seemed plausible. And I wanted his opinion.

I had quite a bit of work to catch up on and didn't come up for air until eleven when there was a knock on the door. When the knob turned, I suddenly realized I hadn't locked it. And whoever it was on the other side wasn't waiting for an invitation.

I stood up as Quentin came in and shut the door behind him. "You did say to come in, didn't you?" He smiled, but there was nothing warm or friendly about it. He had on a pair of tight jeans, a T-shirt and a baggy jacket with big pockets. He looked like a typical college student except for his eyes. They were dark and cold and impenetrable.

"And you are . . .?" I asked, since I wasn't supposed to recognize him from his Facebook page.

He looked uncertain for a moment, then said, "I'm Quentin Davidson. I was in the area, so I thought if now was a good time for you, we could talk here." Without taking his eyes off me for a moment he sat down in the chair in front of my desk.

"Yes, now's a good time," I said as I sat down and reached for my cell. "Just let me text my friend and tell him I'll be a few minutes late for lunch."

Quentin put his hand over my cell phone before I could pick it up. "Isn't it early for lunch?"

"He has a meeting this afternoon," I said, uncertain as to my next move.

"Let's talk first. This might not take long." He moved my cell phone out of reach.

I knew I needed to act natural, but it was hard. "Ah, just let me text my friend," I said, holding my hand out for my phone. As if it had been the most natural thing in the world for him to snatch it up.

"Nice fish," he said, ignoring my outstretched hand. "They don't live long though, do they?"

"They're supposed to," I said, still trying to pretend we were having a normal conversation. "But this is my fourth in under a year."

"I'm not here to hurt you," he said suddenly.

"But you're not here to talk about Blaine's research either, are you?" I might as well name the elephant in the room. It was becoming quite clear that he had an agenda, and I wasn't at all sure it was one I was going to like.

Quentin looked down briefly. My gut said "run," but I didn't know if he had a weapon or not. I would have to keep him talking until I figured out the best move. I waited, letting the silence build, while he made up his mind what he was going to say or do. When he finally spoke, he seemed almost contrite.

"I just want you to understand," he began.

"I'm listening."

"Melissa was everything to my mother. And she was my little sister and my friend. Losing her changed everything, for the family, for me, everything."

"I'm so sorry she couldn't get a transplant," I said.

He became suddenly angry. "She could have had one," he said. "But that fucking doctor and asshole scientist didn't deem her 'worthy.' She was just a statistic to them." He glared at me. "Do you know what it's like to be told that your life isn't worth as much as someone else's? That someone else deserves to live but you don't? Melissa had her whole life ahead of her!" His voice had become loud, out of control. Then his shoulders slumped, and he suddenly became almost subdued.

"She was so special. Loving. Smart. We used to camp out in the back yard. She would make up stories about animals and fairies and going on adventures." He looked out the window as though seeing her reflection out there. "She looked up to me. I was supposed to protect her."

His mood changed again, and his eyes got dark and stormy. "But they kept telling us there was nothing they could do. Everyone refused to help us."

"I know that the medical lists for transplants are compiled by committees," I said, "but I'm surprised that Blaine wasn't willing to experiment." Actually, I wasn't, but it was the only thing I could think of to keep him talking.

"My parents offered to sign disclaimers, to keep the whole thing hush-hush. They just wanted Melissa to have a chance. And Blaine was in the final stages of his research. He could have done it. He could have saved Melissa's life."

He put his hands on the desk and stared at them. I wondered how long it would take him to reach for a concealed weapon if he had one. Maybe this was my only chance to make a break for it. But I waited too long. He withdrew his hands and put them in his pockets. Then he leaned back and took a deep breath as if preparing himself to get down to business.

"I just want you to understand what happened. But you need to back off and leave us alone. Got that?"

I nodded. For a minute I thought he was going to get up and leave, but instead he continued.

"When my buddies and I decided to go hiking in Scotland, I had no idea I was going to run into Blaine. I saw him at a local pub. When he left, I told my friends I wasn't feeling so hot and was going back to our camp to crash. Instead, I followed Blaine to the inn where he was staying. I didn't have a plan; I wasn't even sure I was going to talk to him. Then he saw me and freaked out, so I left. But the next morning I waited for him, and when he came down and got his pack out of his car, I suggested we take a little hike. He thought I had a gun. I didn't, but I let him think that.

"I'd told my buddies I still wasn't feeling so good and would catch up with them later in the day. I didn't anticipate talking to him that long, but things, well, they evolved."

"You don't have to tell me this," I interrupted. I desperately wanted to hear what he had to say, but it didn't seem like it would be healthy for me to do so.

Ignoring my interruption, he said, "I had him drive us to the trailhead. It was pouring. He didn't want to get out of the car, but I insisted. I wanted him to be uncomfortable. I wanted him to be afraid. We hiked up the trail with him in the lead. I could sense he was getting more and more nervous. I told him that Melissa had known she was going to die and how frightened she had been. How his decision had destroyed my family. "He started pleading for his life. Saying he had no choice. The law was very clear. On and on. It was pathetic."

He paused, then added. "I just wanted him to *think* I was going to kill him. I didn't intend to. But he was such a twit. He had absolutely no feeling for what we had gone through. All he could talk about was how he could have lost his job if he had helped us and how important it was for him to complete his project. How it could potentially save thousands of lives.

"He even offered to share the profits with me if I let him go. Can you believe it? He didn't care about anything but his fucking research."

"What happened then?" I asked. I was still afraid, but he had already told me too much, and I was hoping that if I kept him talking long enough, someone might come by. Not likely, but what else was I going to do? I had read enough about brain development to know that as a teenage boy, Quentin's decision-making capabilities weren't completely formed, and he had less control over his emotions and his inhibitions than he would as an adult. Understanding *why* he might have lost control when he ran into Blaine did not, however, help me in the situation I currently found myself in.

"I was going to suggest we head back when he jumped me. It happened so fast. We fought, and he . . . fell. And . . . I . . .

went after him. He kept trying to get away and fell again and again. Then his head hit that rock. I didn't know what to do. Then I saw you standing up there on the trail, and I hid in the trees."

It didn't seem prudent to challenge his story This might be my only chance to convince him I was on his side. "I'm so sorry," I said. "I can only imagine how terrible and confused you must have felt. It was an accident. But given your connection with him, I can understand why you ran away." I couldn't read his face, and I was running out of things to say.

"I'm not going to turn myself in," he said with absolute calm. "It would kill my mother. My parents have suffered enough."

"You don't think the police would understand?"

He stared at me without saying anything for what felt like a long time but was probably only seconds. "I'm not stupid," he said finally. "I know what you're trying to do."

"And what am I trying to do?" That's a negotiation ploy, getting the other side to explain their thinking.

"You want me to think that you won't turn me in."

"I don't want you to go to jail for something that was an accident."

"Then just tell me what you did with Blaine's laptop, and I'll be out of here."

That took me by surprise. "I didn't take his laptop," I said, then instantly regretted it. Maybe I could have strung him along.

"Then what happened to it?"

"I thought maybe whoever was in the ravine took it. But if that was you, and you don't have it, well I wish I knew, but I don't."

He leaned forward. "I can't get away without money," he said.

"How much do you need?" I asked.

"More than *you* have."

"So, what can I do?"

He suddenly pounded my desk with his fist. "You can give me the fucking laptop."

Everything was suddenly coming together. "How much have they offered you?"

"It's worth a lot of money," he said with emotion. "A lot."

"Think, Quentin. Even if I'd found it in Blaine's backpack, I wouldn't have held onto it. I would have turned it over to the Mountain Rescue Team. I had no idea what was on it."

He stared at me a moment, then stood up. "Come on," he said. "We're going out to your boat."

I remained seated. "Why?" I was pretty sure I knew the answer, but I was praying that I was wrong.

He pulled out a gun. "This time I came prepared. Now get up and let's go." He put the gun back in his pocket but kept his hand on it.

"You're making things worse," I said. "Your parents will understand about your fight with Blaine, but this doesn't make any sense."

"I just want to make sure you don't have his laptop," he said.

"You're too late. Someone already searched my office, my locker, my parents' house, and my boat." No one had searched my boat, although someone had tried. If Quentin had been responsible for these searches, my boat would still be a place he would want to check out.

"I want to take a look for myself. So, let's go. Just stay to my right and we'll walk out there together, side by side, okay?" I didn't see that I had any choice, but my mind was in overdrive, trying desperately to come up with something. Was there even the slightest possibility that he would let me go when he didn't find a laptop on my boat? What could I possibly do to escape without getting shot?

At the bottom of the stairs he started down the dock toward where my boat is usually moored, and I had to point out that I'd moved it. That seemed to unsettle him, but it didn't change his plan. We headed down the other dock, me staying to his right as directed so he could use the gun in his pocket if necessary.

It was one of Logan's non-teaching days. He had said he was

going to run errands and return after lunch, so it was far too early for him to come to my rescue. And there are seldom many people around the marina in the middle of the day during the week. The only person we saw as we headed out the dock was someone I didn't recognize. He ignored my eye gestures and my subtly mouthed "help" and kept right on going. Once he was out of sight I said, "He'll be able to identify you."

Quentin didn't respond. I wasn't sure if that meant he didn't care or if he intended to be long gone by the time anyone discovered my body.

We climbed over the *Carpe Diem* and onto the aft deck of the *Aspara*, ducking under the tarp. It's a small space to begin with and feels even smaller with the tarp cover. I'd put the cover back as soon as we'd returned. I like the privacy. But at the moment, it wasn't privacy that I needed.

Quentin stepped aboard right after me and stood behind me in the cockpit while I unlocked the padlock. Then I braced myself as I slid back the hatch.

An orange ball of fur catapulted out of the boat and streaked past us. Quentin was startled and took an unsteady step back as I whirled around and kicked him in the crotch. This was not the first time Macavity had pulled this little stunt after being trapped inside, and I'd been praying he would do exactly what he had just done. Earlier I had cleaned some bird poop off of Macavity's porthole and had closed it to do some polishing that I'd failed to get around to. For once good intentions and procrastination paid off.

Before he had a chance to recover, I kicked Quentin a second time in the balls while screaming my head off. Then I kicked him in the head and in the neck and anywhere I could aim my foot, screaming all the while.

He was gagging and trying to reach for the gun he had dropped, but I beat him to it.

"Stay down," I ordered as he seemed about to get up. "I'll shoot you in the kneecap," I said, aiming the gun at his knee.

"Bitch," he said, his voice barely audible, but his venom came through loud and clear. Underdeveloped amygdala be damned; he was a most unpleasant young man.

I tried to back up so I could give him room to stand up without giving him a chance to turn the tables on me, but it is such a cramped space I decided it was best to keep him where he was. I screamed, "Anyone out there? I need help on the *Aspara*."

No one answered.

He started to move again.

"We're going to stay right where we are until someone comes." I resisted saying *make my day*. Instead I said, "Don't move and you'll live to pay for what you did to Blaine."

I was shaking all over, but now that I was in control, I was also feeling just a tiny bit sorry for him. "For the record," I said, "I don't think you meant to kill him. And I do think Melissa got a bum deal. And I'm very sad for your parents." Then I added,

"And I *don't* and never did have Blaine's laptop, tablet or a thumb drive with the data on it. I have no idea what happened to his data. But I do know that someone searched his room at the inn. Was that you?"

"No." He seemed surprised. "I didn't think of that. I was sure you had taken whatever was in the backpack."

"Anyone out there?" I yelled again as loud as I could. "I need help on the *Aspara*." When no one answered, we continued our conversation, as if he wasn't on the floor of my cockpit and I didn't have a gun pointed at him. "So, if it wasn't you, who else knew that Blaine was even in the area? Did you mention it to your friends?"

"No way. I didn't want to get them involved."

"Nice of you," I said. "But you did tell someone that I had the information."

"Yes. I needed the money."

"How did you find someone interested?" I wasn't sure he would tell me, but he seemed almost eager to talk.

"I asked around. Mom and Dad and I had made contact with quite a few people who make organs available for a price. One of them put me in touch with someone who was extremely inter-ested in what Blaine was working on. A rival company, I think."

"Was it you who called the inn and told them Blaine was extending his vacation?"

"No, I think the people I was negotiating with did. They wanted to give me time to locate his computer."

"Well, you certainly got in bed with some dangerous people. Unless you got a friend to help you beat up Conrad." I could tell he was starting to feel more confident, so I kept the gun pointed directly at his knee, nice and steady.

"Who's Conrad?" He sounded sincerely puzzled.

"But you did stab my goldfish."

"It was just a fish. I wanted you to back off."

His attitude toward Bubbles drained some of the sympathy

I was feeling for him. "Anyone out there?" I screamed at the top of my lungs, "I need help on the *Aspara*."

"Bryn, is that you?" I heard Logan calling. Then I heard him running across the *Carpe Diem* toward us.

"I'm okay, Logan," I yelled. "But I've got company."

He peered under the tarp and saw me with a gun pointed at Quentin. "Call Ben," I said. "And tell him to hurry."

"no one like macavity"

That evening we had a celebration aboard the *Carpe Diem*. Logan, Judd, Sophie, Ben, and me. Ben had reprimanded me for not calling him to follow up on Quentin, but we had quickly moved on. The rest of us were all incredibly pleased that we were going to be able to come and go without looking over our shoulders. And I was happy that the *Aspara* was back home.

As for Macavity, he had no idea that he had played such a critical role in capturing Quentin. He had undoubtedly assumed he was going to have to go through a prolonged period of captivity all over again and had simply acted out his aggression in his usual way, living up to the description in the T.S. Eliot poem:

Macavity, Macavity, there's no one like Macavity, He's broken every human law, he breaks the law of gravity.

We had just reached the bottom of our first bottle of wine when my phone rang. It was Fiona. "You won't believe this," she began. She explained that she'd had an anonymous tip about who had taken Blaine's research. "I don't know why they called me," she said. "I'm just glad they did."

I had a pretty good idea who the tipster was, and it made sense to me that Keith would have called Fiona. He knew she'd follow up and put pressure on the authorities to act. And he also knew that she would not confuse the murder with the theft. Of course, he had no way of knowing at the time who the murderer was.

"Poor Rory," she said. "He didn't know why Blaine hadn't shown up for their meeting and had gone to the inn to see what was happening. When there was no answer, he was about to leave, but the maid showed up. On the spur of the moment he decided to take advantage of the situation. He asked the maid if she could let him into his room; said he'd left the key inside. She was happy to do so. He looks so normal, she didn't even question him. He said he wasn't sure what he intended to do. It wasn't like him to lie like that. Then he saw the laptop, tablet, and thumb all right out in the open on the desk.

"Our theory is that Blaine ran down to get something out of his car and intended to come right back but was waylaid. By someone. Or something happened. We don't know why he ended up on the trail."

"Your theory is most likely correct," I said. "I think he may have gone to his car for his backpack or something that was in it. And I know what happened after that." Then it was my turn to explain. When I was done, we agreed that it was a sad story with an even sadder ending for the Davidsons. On the other hand, Fiona was happy for me. Happy that I was alive, happy that I had finally discovered what had happened, and happy that I would be able to move on.

I had gone out on the back deck to talk, but the sounds of laughter suddenly rose to a crescendo. "What's going on there?" Fiona asked. I explained that we were celebrating and that her news would result in at least one more bottle of wine being opened.

"I'm just glad all of the loose ends have been tied up," I said. "I hate unfinished puzzles."

"Want to know what makes me happy?" Fiona asked. "The day they finally found Blaine, my fellow rescue team members were forced to concede you had been right all along, about the location and about the body."

I laughed. "Wish I'd been there to see their faces. By the way, what did your scientist do with the devices?" "He says he wiped them and then destroyed them."

"Did he take a peek first?"

"Claims he didn't. Said they were password protected. He just wanted to slow Blaine's work down a bit. Maybe talk some sense into him about following protocols."

"Do you believe him?"

Fiona thought for a moment. "I think so. He is really concerned about the potential consequences of this kind of research. I think he wanted to make a point. And, of course, he didn't know that Blaine was dead."

"Will he be prosecuted?"

"If I had to guess, I'd say they will work out a deal with him. Unless NorPac puts up a fuss."

"They may not want the publicity," I said. "The headlines could make them look bad: 'Ethical Scottish scientist destroys data of reckless American researcher.' Or, something like that. If the data is truly gone, they may just want to move on."

We ended our conversation on a happy note, and I went back inside to tell the others about Fiona's news. Everyone immediately started debating about whether Rory had taken a peek or made a copy of Blaine's research. I felt the speculation said more about us than about what might really have happened. What can I say—there is no way I wouldn't have taken a peek. And there was no way Mr. Straight Arrow Judd would have. He wouldn't have gone into the room under false pretenses in the first place, so he wouldn't have had the opportunity. Sophie argued both sides, sometimes simultaneously. Logan, well, Logan and I are soul mates. The only one who surprised me was Ben. Although he didn't come right out and say it, I think he approved of Rory's actions. Now if he would just shave off the mustache—

As he was leaving, Ben handed me a small box. "What is it?" I asked.

"Just a memento, something I saw in a window that made me think of you."

I opened it up, not knowing what to expect. Inside was a silver chimera on a chain—the head of a goat, body of a lion, and tail of a dragon. "This makes you think of me?" I said. I didn't know whether to laugh or cry. Other women get diamonds or pearls. Or roses or chocolates. But I get a chimera on a chain.

Why me?

Thank you for reading *Why Me? Chimeras, Conundrums and Dead Goldfish*. I hope you enjoyed it. The next two in the series are:

Who Me? Fog Bows, Fraud and Aphrodite (A Macavity & Me Mystery #2)

Not Me! Speluncaphobia, Secrets and Hidden Treasure (A Macavity & Me Mystery #3)

Other books by Charlotte Stuart include:

The Discount Detective Mysteries
The John Smith Mysteries
Bogged Down (A Vashon Island Mystery)
Raven's Grave
Midnight for Justice, a legal thriller by Charlotte Stuart and Don Stuart

Acknowledgments

I want to thank Mary Custureri and Donna Eastman for giving the first edition of this series a chance. I also want to thank readers who encouraged me by saying that they can relate to Bryn as a person and share my fondness for Macavity. In addition, I feel fortunate to have had the help of Sue Trowbridge and Christine Holmes in adapting the original manuscripts for the second edition. Finally, I am forever grateful to my number one reader and editor, Don.

About the Author

Award-winning author Charlotte Stuart PhD writes mysteries that fall into a number of different sub genres: cozy mysteries, character-driven mysteries featuring a female PI, a laugh-out-loud comedic series, as well more traditional mysteries. She's also co-authored a legal thriller with Don Stuart. In general, she favors twisty plots with a dollop of adventure.

Before she started writing full time, she left a tenured faculty position to go commercial salmon fishing in Alaska, spent a year sailing "around the world" in the Washington and Canadian San Juans, became a partner in a management consulting group and later a VP of HR and Training. After living on boats for over a decade, boating and forays into wilderness areas often find their way into her stories.

Why Me? Chimeras, Conundrums and Dead Goldfish is the first in the Macavity & Me Mysteries. It won a Global eBook gold and was a NYC Big Book Distinguished Favorite.

Charlotte lives on Vashon Island in the Pacific Northwest and is the past president of the Puget Sound Sisters in Crime and a member of the Mystery Writers of America and the International Thriller Writers.

You can visit her website at www.charlottestuart.com, or contact her on social media:

facebook.com/charlotte.stuart.mysterywriter

instagram.com/cstuartauthor

bookbub.com/authors/charlotte-stuart

goodreads.com/goodreadscomclstuart